A portal to another world...

The chest was empty except for some dead insects. At first Anthony was disappointed, and he was about to close the lid when something stopped him. From inside the chest a whispering sound came. It was like many voices talking together, saying words that he couldn't understand. Anthony felt like someone who is hypnotized—he couldn't tear himself away. Now, as he stared into the old wooden box, the bottom filled with writhing curls of smoke. Then the smoke cleared, and blackness opened before him. It seemed to Anthony that he was looking down into a bottomless pit. Gripping the sides of the box, he went on staring, but then he began to feel that he was going to be drawn over the

"T   is
ap   r-
so   al

"E   to
th   A

Discover the Terrifying World of
John Bellairs!

Johnny Dixon Mysteries

The Bell, the Book, and the Spellbinder

The Chessmen of Doom

The Curse of the Blue Figurine

The Drum, the Doll, and the Zombie

The Eyes of the Killer Robot

The Hand of the Necromancer

The Mummy, the Will, and the Crypt

The Revenge of the Wizard's Ghost

The Secret of the Underground Room

The Spell of the Sorcerer's Skull

The Trolley to Yesterday

The Wrath of the Grinning Ghost

Lewis Barnavelt Mysteries

The Beast Under the Wizard's Bridge
The Doom of the Haunted Opera
The Figure in the Shadows
The Ghost in the Mirror
The House With a Clock in Its Walls
The Letter, the Witch, and the Ring
The Specter from the Magician's Museum
The Tower at the End of the World
The Vengeance of the Witch-Finder
The Whistle, the Grave, and the Ghost

Anthony Monday Mysteries

The Dark Secret of Weatherend
The Lamp from the Warlock's Tomb
The Mansion in the Mist
The Treasure of Alpheus Winterborn

The Mansion
in the Mist

JOHN BELLAIRS

Frontispiece
by Edward Gorey

PUFFIN BOOKS

PUFFIN BOOKS
Published by Penguin Group
Penguin Young Readers Group,
345 Hudson Street, New York, New York 10014, U.S.A.
Penguin Books Ltd, 80 Strand, London WC2R ORL, England
Penguin Books Australia Ltd, 250 Camberwell Road, Camberwell, Victoria 3124, Australia
Penguin Books Canada Ltd, 10 Alcorn Avenue, Toronto, Ontario, Canada M4V 3B2
Penguin Books (N.Z.) Ltd, 182-190 Wairau Road, Auckland 10, New Zealand

First published in the United States of America by Dial Books for Young Readers,
a division of Penguin Books USA Inc.,1992
Published by Puffin Books, 1993
Reissued by Puffin Books, a division of Penguin Young Readers Group, 2004

1 3 5 7 9 10 8 6 4 2

LIBRARY OF CONGRESS CATALOGING-IN-PUBLICATION DATA
Bellairs, John.
The mansion in the mist / by John Bellairs; frontispiece by Edward Gorey.
p. cm.
Summary: While spending the summer in an old house on a desolate Canadian island,
Anthony Monday and Miss Eells discover a chest that can transport them to another
world and a maniacal group who are plotting the destruction of people on Earth.
ISBN 0-14-034933-2
[1. Mystery and detective stories. 2. Magic—Fiction.]
I. Gorey, Edward, 1925– ill. II. Title.
[PZ7. B413Man 1993] [Fic]—dc20 92-44005 CIP AC

This edition ISBN 0-14-240262-1

Printed in the United States of America

The Mansion
in the Mist

CHAPTER ONE

"But, Miss Eells! It's gonna be really crummy with you gone for the summer! I don't get along with Miss Pratt, and . . . well, *you* know."

Anthony Monday and his friend Miss Eells were sitting on a wooden bench, which was perched atop a high embankment in Levee Park in the city of Hoosac, Minnesota. It was a mild day in May, in the mid-1950's, and the waters of the Mississippi River were rippled by a stiff flowery-smelling breeze. Anthony was a tall gawky-looking young man of thirteen. He was wearing a red leather cap with a scrunched peak, a red plaid shirt with a buttoned pocket, gray corduroy pants, and white suede shoes. Miss Eells was an odd little woman close to seventy years old, with bright, darting birdlike eyes, gold-rimmed glasses, and a wild mess of white hair. She was the head librarian of the public library in Hoosac, and Anthony worked for her as a page. They had known each other for several years, and they had a strange but wonderful friendship: Anthony told Miss Eells things about himself that he would never have told anyone else, because he trusted and believed in her. Miss Eells was kind to Anthony, but—most important of all—she was a good listener. In spite of their friendship, however, a problem had arisen lately: Miss Eells had decided to go on vacation for two months in the summer. It was her first vacation in fifteen years, and she was planning to spend it with her brother Emerson at his rambling old cottage on an island in northern Canada. But Miss Eells's plans had left Anthony feeling like a fish out of water. He didn't have any close friends his own age, and so he depended on Miss Eells to get him through the long boring months of summer, when there was nothing much to do except go to the movies, play tetherball, and sit in front of the TV set like a zombie. On the other hand, Anthony couldn't very well tell his old friend to stay home—he knew that she deserved a vacation. He just wished that he was going away with her.

Miss Eells stared into the muddy waters of the river that lay below them. She puckered up her mouth and looked discontented. "Anthony," she began slowly, "there is a solution to our problem, but I'm not sure it's one that would work out. I could ask Emerson to invite you to come along, but I don't know if you'd be happy in his rickety old house on that godforsaken chilly lake. There's no electricity, no TV, and the nearest settlement is ten miles across the lake by motorboat. I'm just afraid that you'd be terribly bored. Do you see what I mean?"

Anthony shook his head stubbornly. "No, Miss Eells, I really wouldn't be bored. My mom says I mope around in the summertime like a lost Charlie Ross, whatever that means. I think it would be fun to go away with you and Emerson."

Miss Eells shifted her feet restlessly, stirring the pile of dead leaves that lay in front of the bench. "You can be very persuasive, Anthony," she began, "but still—"

"And besides," said Anthony, cutting in, "Miss Pratt doesn't like to have me working for her. She's always crabbing at me and telling me to do some work for a change. You know what I mean, don't you?"

Miss Eells sighed and smiled ruefully. "I will admit that Miss Pratt's personality could be improved upon," she said. "Look, I'll tell you what I'm going to do: I'll call Emerson and ask him if you can go along. But in the meantime you've got to do two things. First, you have to get your parents' permission, and then you've got to round up somebody to sub for you at the library. Do you think you can do that?"

Anthony said yes and nodded enthusiastically. That evening, Miss Eells called up her brother, who was only too happy to have Anthony come along on the trip. Anthony got his parents to let him go, and after a few phone calls Anthony got hold of Ted Hoopenbecker, a red-haired kid who sometimes played Ping-Pong and pool with him down at the YMCA, and he agreed to fill in at the library. So everything got arranged, after all. A week before their trip was going to start, Emerson Eells came down to Hoosac to visit his sister. Emerson was a rabbitty looking little man with a fluff of white hair on his head. He was a rich lawyer who lived in St. Cloud, and he always dressed very well. He drove a black 1938 LaSalle, which was a bit eccentric, but that was Emerson. And though Emerson was a little pompous and a know-it-all, he liked Anthony and respected him for his courage and forthrightness. Most of the time, the two of them got along fine.

It was a chilly evening, and rain was falling. Emerson sat on Miss Eells's living room sofa and puffed at one of his fancy meerschaum pipes. Miss Eells sat across from him in an armchair, sipping tea and trying not to spill any of it. And perched on a kitchen chair nearby sat Anthony. He had a bottle of Coke in his hand and he looked uncomfortable, as he often did in the presence of some older people. Emerson was rambling on about the trip they were going to take in a few days, and he had just dropped a hint that there might be a mysterious jack-in-the-box waiting for them at the old cottage in Canada.

Miss Eells set down her teacup, slopping some into

the saucer. "A jack-in-the-box?" she said nervously. "I hope you don't mean something unpleasant—I was hoping to have a nice, restful time up there."

Anthony, however, was excited by the possibility of a mystery. "What do you mean by that, Mr. Eells?" he asked, leaning forward.

Emerson smoked placidly and smiled. He enjoyed being tantalizing. "Well, there may be nothing to this," he began, as he blew a smoke ring into the air, "but—as Myra well knows—there is a riddle to be solved. You see, a few years ago I rented the cottage to some tourists who wanted a couple of weeks of roughing it out in the wild. Apparently they got more than they bargained for, because all three of them disappeared!"

Anthony's eyes grew wide. "Disappeared? Really?"

Emerson nodded. "Yes, really. One day when the farmer who lives across the lake arrived with the weekly supply of butter, eggs, and bacon, he found that the cottage was deserted. The rowboat was still tied up to the dock, so the tourists couldn't have left that way, and besides, they left their clothes and other belongings behind. To this day no one knows what happened to them."

"And Emerson thinks he'll find the three of them buried in shallow graves somewhere on the island," put in Miss Eells with a malicious grin.

"Mock all you want to, Myra," Emerson said as he knocked out his pipe into an ashtray. "But I will bet you five dollars that we will find some clue to their disappearance when we go up there. At any rate, I'm going to have a look around."

Anthony's eyes shone. Secretly he hoped that Emerson would find something—something not too frightening, but exciting all the same.

CHAPTER TWO

⁓⁂⁓

The pontoon plane glided to a smooth landing on the
choppy waters of Shadow Lake. Peering out the small
square window, Anthony saw steep ranks of trees rising
solemnly on all sides. Straight ahead, a long white dock
jutted out from the shore, and behind it rose a large
cottage with shingled sides and a steeply pitched roof
covered with slates. Two tall brick chimneys rose from
the roof, and there was a screened porch. On the second
story, a tiny balcony overhung the porch. The place
looked totally deserted—as indeed it was for most of the
year. To Anthony there seemed to be something forbidding about the place, as if it was warning him not to
come any closer.

"Well, here we are," said Emerson quietly, as the plane

stopped next to the dock. He had been very cheerful about this trip at the beginning, but now that he was here he didn't sound all that enthusiastic.

Emerson thanked the pilot, and they all tramped down the gangplank to the dock with their luggage. Then the plane started its motors again, did a U-turn, and sped off down the long lake for a takeoff. Curiously Anthony was sorry to see the plane go. He felt that they were being abandoned. But he shrugged off his fears, and whistling cheerfully, he threw his duffel bag over his shoulder and followed Emerson and Miss Eells down the dock to the silent, waiting house.

For the next two days, the three vacationers spent their time getting the cottage into shape. They found that the living conditions were pretty old-fashioned: There was no electricity, so they got light from six oil lamps with shiny metal reflectors mounted on them. Water came from a bubbling rock spring not far from the back door of the house, and instead of a refrigerator there was an icehouse, a little gray wooden shed full of blocks of ice. Emerson had ordered the ice a few days before, and a man would be coming around once a week to refill the supply. Also there was a pest problem: The house had been taken over by black beetles and mice, and Emerson spent a lot of time setting mousetraps and spraying the baseboards of the rooms with Flit, a popular bug killer. In spite of these problems, the three campers pitched in and worked: Anthony polished the reflectors and filled the lamps with kerosene. Dishes got washed, tables were scrubbed, windows got Windexed, and floors were mopped. Finally things seemed to be in decent order, and the vacationers decided that they could sit back and enjoy themselves.

Days passed, and Anthony began to feel the pleasure of being in the great Canadian north woods. He loved the weird cries of the loons at night, and the occasional sound of a tree crashing down in the wilderness. Emerson taught Anthony to fish with a bamboo rod and a line. It wasn't as exciting as fly casting, but it was restful, and you almost always caught something. Miss Eells didn't fish, but she would sit in the boat and knit or read long novels by Charles Dickens. At night, the three of them gathered in the living room of the cottage, lit the six lamps, and played pinochle. Or Emerson might bang away at the old upright piano. Some nights they listened to music on Emerson's big battery-powered radio. The pleasures of this kind of life were quiet, but everybody seemed contented.

Toward the end of the first week of their stay, Anthony began to feel that there was something wrong about the house. Nothing that you could get a grip on, but still something, well, *wrong.* One night he woke during a wild thunderstorm, and the boards in the corridor outside his bedroom were creaking loudly. Lightning leapt in through the tiny window, and loud cracking peals of thunder burst overhead. But it was the creaking that bothered Anthony—it sounded like people walking up and down. When he finally got up his courage, he opened the door and peered out. Nobody there. The doors to Miss Eells's and Emerson's bedrooms were shut, and they were probably asleep. Timidly, Anthony crept down the front staircase and peered into the shadowy living room. As his eyes got used to the dark, he saw something that froze his blood: Someone was sitting in one of the rockers. Anthony clenched his teeth and closed his eyes. He could hear his heart hammering. Then he opened his eyes again, and a blue flash of lightning lit the room. The dark shape was gone.

For a long time Anthony stood in the doorway, staring into darkness. Then he groped his way to a table and found a box of matches to light a lamp. The smoky yellowish glow showed that the room was empty. Anyone who tried to leave the room would have had to brush past Anthony. Also, there would have been footsteps, and Anthony did not hear any. A chill spread from his feet to his tingling scalp. What had he seen? Finally, after his fear had died down, Anthony trudged back up the stairs and threw himself into bed.

A couple of days later something else happened that was odd and unexplainable. Miss Eells and Emerson had taken the rowboat over to the settlement across the lake, so they could pick up some supplies. Anthony was alone in the house. For a while he sat on the end of the dock and waggled his feet in the water, while Emerson's portable radio played nearby. Then he rolled up his pants and waded for a while in the chilly water, but after a few minutes his feet began to sting, so he climbed back onto the splintery slats. The sun sank low, and with a towel tied around his waist, Anthony padded back up to the house and warmed himself in front of the fireplace. When he was all dry and warm again he sat on the porch and played his harmonica. This was something he was just learning to do, and most of the time he got awful squawky sounds, but he struggled on nevertheless. At last, as the sun was setting, he got tired of playing and went back into the house to explore.

He was beginning to feel uneasy about Emerson and Miss Eells, but he remembered that Miss Eells could be a fussy shopper. And both of his friends could get so wrapped up in bickering with each other that they lost track of time. It wouldn't hurt, Anthony decided, to keep himself busy by having a good look around. He took a kerosene lamp with him and headed upstairs.

The bedrooms there were all alike: small and rather homely. The walls were knotty pine, and the floors were covered with reed rugs. The beds were iron Army cots, and next to each one was a chair to hang your clothes on. The only decoration the rooms had were framed pictures made out of colored yarn. Anthony walked aimlessly from room to room. He wasn't really looking for anything in particular—he was just killing time till his friends came back. He looked out the window of one bedroom and saw that the stars were beginning to twinkle in the sky, but he saw no sign of the rowboat.

Finally he reached a room at the end of the corridor, a room that was different from the rest. There was no bed in it, and the floor was very dusty. A sleepy fly buzzed and bumped stupidly against the dirty window-panes. In the center of the floor stood a large wooden chest. It was made of rough unvarnished wood, and a yellowed label had once been stuck to the lid, but some-one had ripped it off so that only a fragment remained. Curious, Anthony knelt next to the chest and raised the lid. The hinges groaned, and a smell of raw wood rose to Anthony's nostrils. He looked in.

The chest was empty except for some dead insects. At first Anthony was disappointed, and he was about to close the lid when something stopped him. From in-side the chest a whispering sound came. It was like many voices talking together, saying words that he couldn't understand. Anthony felt like someone who is hypno-tized—he couldn't tear himself away. Now, as he stared into the old wooden box, the bottom filled with writh-ing curls of smoke. Then the smoke cleared, and black-ness opened before him. It seemed to Anthony that he was looking down into a bottomless pit. Gripping the sides of the box, he went on staring, but then he began to feel the growing urge to clamber over the sides of the chest and throw himself in. At the last minute he pulled back with a shudder of fear. Down came the lid with a loud slam, and Anthony hauled himself to his feet with a mighty effort. Staggering like a drunken person, he reeled out through the doorway and collapsed in a dead faint on the hall floor.

CHAPTER THREE

Night was deepening on the lake as Emerson and Miss Eells came drifting up to the dock in their rowboat. Anthony was sitting on the end of the dock with his back toward his two friends. From the darkness Emerson called out, "Sorry to be so late, my boy, but Graceful Gertie here tried her hand at piloting us. First she ran us onto a rock and bent the propeller of my outboard motor, and then she managed to break both our oars. We had to paddle back to town with our hands to buy a new set. Did you miss us?"

Sitting next to his lighted lantern, Anthony did not turn around or respond to Emerson's call. After a quick worried glance at Anthony, Emerson tied the boat up to a post and held it close to the dock so Miss Eells could jump out. Then he lunged out himself, did a barrel roll across the dock, and sprang nimbly to his feet. He and Miss Eells walked slowly toward Anthony. They stopped just behind him, and Emerson coughed and tried to look cheerful.

"Hem!" he said, as he reached down and gave Anthony a little pat on the back. "Are you getting interested in Buddhist meditation, my boy? If so, you should be sitting cross-legged and not waggling your feet in the—"

Emerson's voice died away when Anthony turned to face him. The yellow lantern light revealed Anthony's tear-streaked face. He looked utterly, totally miserable.

"What in the name of . . ." began Emerson, but he cut himself off. Then, more gently he added, "What's wrong, son?"

"I . . . I saw something awful," Anthony began haltingly. "It . . . it . . ." But he couldn't go on.

Miss Eells stepped forward. Stooping, she gave Anthony her arm and helped him to his feet. "Come on, Tony," she said softly. "Emerson, you bring the groceries. Let's go up to the cottage and have a talk."

A few minutes later, the three of them were sitting in the living room. The six oil lamps burned brightly, and the potbellied stove in the corner took away the evening chill. Anthony was sitting in a rocking chair with a glass of ginger ale in his hand. He still looked confused and half asleep, but the color was returning to his cheeks. Emerson and Miss Eells sat nearby. They frowned anxiously and kept glancing at the floor, as if they couldn't quite think of what they ought to say. Finally Emerson broke the silence.

"Anthony, my boy," he said quietly, "it's terrible to see you in this state. But it'll be better for you if you can tell us what happened. Was there a burglar here? Or are you homesick?"

Anthony shook his head. "No, Mr. Eells, it's . . . It's not like that at all. Like I said, I saw something awful." Then, haltingly Anthony began to tell about the mysterious whispering chest. But he was only just halfway through his story when Emerson cut him off.

"Anthony!" he exclaimed. "This is incredible! I know this house as well as I know the back of my hand, and there isn't any chest in that room—or anywhere else in the house for that matter."

Anthony stared in amazement. Could Emerson be telling the truth? Carefully, Anthony set his empty glass down on a table. "Could . . . could we go up and look right now?" he asked in a faltering voice.

Emerson stared for a second and then he smiled confidently. "Of course we can!" he said as he sprang to his feet. Grabbing an oil lamp, Emerson motioned for the others to follow him. They went up the dark stairs single file and down the long corridor. The lamp cast weird shadows on the wall as they moved along, and through the open windows you could hear the wind hissing in the pines. At the far end of the hall, they paused outside the room that Anthony had mentioned.

Emerson went in first, with the lamp held high in his hand, and the others followed him. The wavering smoky light showed that the room was empty.

Anthony felt sick. He put his hand to his forehead and closed his eyes. A fit of dizziness came over him, and he shook his head violently. "It . . . it really was there," he muttered weakly. "Honest, it was!"

Emerson eyed him skeptically. "Anthony, my boy," he said, "has it occurred to you that maybe you fell asleep and dreamed the whole thing?"

Anthony looked disgusted. "Come on, Mr. Eells! I know when I'm asleep and when I'm awake! I really did see this big wooden chest, and it was right here where we're standing. Honest!"

"Well, in that case," put in Miss Eells calmly, "we have a mystery on our hands. I believe you saw something, Anthony, and if Emerson here wasn't such a know-it-all he'd agree with me. To tell the truth, I've felt that there was something creepy about this house ever since I first set foot in it. Em, do you think we should go home?"

Emerson shook his head vigorously. "Absolutely not! In the first place, I want to find out what happened to those three people I rented this place to. And in the second place, I'm not going to be scared off by tales of disappearing chests. Besides I enjoy the fishing and the whole relaxing atmosphere of this island."

"Relaxing!" snorted Miss Eells. "We'll see how relaxing things will be if more strange things happen." But she knew there was not much point in arguing further with her stubborn brother, so she gave up and went downstairs to the living room with the others. Emerson banged out some ragtime on the piano while Anthony and Miss Eells played cards. After a short time they all got very drowsy and went off to bed, and Anthony fell asleep to the sound of water gurgling over stones outside his window.

Days passed, and nothing very exciting happened. Emerson found an old badminton set tucked away in a closet, and he set it up in the side yard. The three of them took turns playing one another, and they had a lot of fun. Anthony caught a few fish, but because they were small Emerson made him throw them back. Gradually everybody got used to life on the island, and for the most part they found it enjoyable and relaxing. Yet, the chest and the disappearing figure stayed on Anthony's mind—he couldn't quite get rid of them.

One still, muggy afternoon, while Emerson and Miss Eells were out fishing, Anthony began wandering about the house again. For the first time in days he was really beginning to feel bored. He poked into closets and found old croquet sets, bows and arrows, warped golf clubs, and one dead mouse. Then he went downstairs and decided to examine the small pantry that was next to the kitchen. On its dusty shelves he found old cloudy jars of preserves that probably weren't fit to eat, a tin pail that had once held Swift's lard, an inkwell, and an old wooden pen holder with a rusty metal nib. There was also a brown earthenware jug and an old meat grinder that was missing its handle. Anthony was about to leave when he noticed the glimmer of something white behind one of the jars of preserves. Reaching in, he pulled out a fan-shaped vase made of milky white china. Turning it upside down, he shook out a small white card. It was covered with dust, but when he had blown the dust away Anthony saw that there was writing on the card in copper-colored ink. It took him a while to figure out what the handwriting said, but finally it became clear:

> The password: Auro est locus in quo conflatur. And the greatest clue of all is in the Temple of the Winds.

Anthony stared at the card. He hardly knew what to think. What could this mean? Password? Password for what? He didn't know Latin, so he didn't have the faintest idea what the mysterious phrase meant. And the second sentence was pure gibberish as far as he was concerned. Nevertheless, puzzles fascinated Anthony, and he took the card away with him. He would show it to Emerson and see if he could make anything out of it.

Later that afternoon, when Emerson and Miss Eells came back, Anthony showed them the card. Like Anthony, Emerson had trouble with the handwriting, but he figured it out eventually. With a little shrug and an odd smirk, he handed the card back to Anthony.

"It's as clear as mud!" sighed Emerson. "The Latin phrase is from the Book of Job in the Bible. It means:

There is a place for gold where it is gathered together. Good news for prospectors, I suppose, but not very helpful to anyone else. As for the second phrase, I have to agree with you—it's utterly meaningless. At one time rich people owned vast estates, and they built little ornamental buildings on the grounds just to pretty things up. Sometimes the buildings had names like the Temple of the Winds. But we don't have anything like that here. You know what I think? Some people who were vacationing here long ago played charades at night, and these were two of the phrases that people had to act out. And when you consider the Latin phrase, they were probably a bunch of professors. I wouldn't spend any time mulling over that card if I were you, Anthony—you'll just be driving yourself buggy over nothing. It's not a clue to help you find a gold mine or anything like that. Tear it up and sleep well tonight!"

Anthony nodded politely to Emerson and stuck the crumpled card in his pocket. In his heart he was not convinced by Emerson's wonderful explanation, but he didn't feel like arguing.

The rest of the day was spent playing badminton and pinochle and arguing over baseball trivia. After the sun went down the three campers sat in rocking chairs on the front porch and watched the twilight deepen over Shadow Lake and the stars come out. An ominous silence spread over the water, and in the west a dark thunderhead was rising.

"I think a storm is coming on," said Emerson, as he puffed at his meerschaum pipe. "And I'll bet it's going to be a real gully washer."

"You're such a great weather forecaster," said Miss Eells. "You ought to be on television."

"Isn't she wonderful, Anthony?" Emerson chortled. "And to think I've had to put up with her for more than sixty years. It's a wonder I haven't turned into an ax murderer or a mad strangler."

"There's still time," muttered Miss Eells, and then she burst into a fit of giggles.

Throughout all this kidding Anthony sat in stony silence. He was thinking of the mysterious disappearing chest. What if it returned to the empty room tonight? He hoped that it wouldn't. He really didn't want to see the thing again, ever. The trouble was, he couldn't get the chest out of his mind—it was burning a hole in his brain. What was it for? Did the password have anything to do with it? Every time he asked himself these questions his head ached.

The stormy darkness on the lake deepened. A jagged streak of lightning split the sky, and thunder rumbled in the distance. A cold wind began to blow, and the three campers went inside for more pinochle. Miss Eells had baked some peanut butter cookies in the oven of the old iron cookstove, and they were delicious. Everybody guzzled ginger ale, talked a lot, argued over points, and had a good time. Finally the old shelf clock in the kitchen whanged eleven times, and everyone began to yawn.

"Well, I guess it's sleepy time," sighed Miss Eells, as she gathered the cards together and stacked them neatly in the middle of the table. "There's one thing, you know, that's good about roughing it in the wilderness: If a storm hits, it can't knock out your power, because there isn't any."

"You always see the bright side of things," sniffed Emerson. "Next year I am going to have a generator installed up here. It won't be picturesque, but at least we won't ruin our eyes trying to read by oil lamplight."

One by one, Emerson, Miss Eells, and Anthony made their way to the table at the foot of the stairs. On it were three candles in brass holders, and several small boxes of matches. Everyone lit a candle and plodded wearily off to bed. But when Anthony got to the door of his room, he felt wide awake and tense. He sat down on the edge of his bed and tried to calm his beating heart, but in spite of all his efforts he still felt as if he was ready to jump out of his skin. *What was he so worked up about?* And then it hit him: the password, the Latin phrase he had found in the old dusty vase. What was it for? He had an idea now, a strange and fascinating idea. When he knelt over the old wooden chest in the back room, he felt that the swirling mists hid a doorway. A doorway to . . . to where? He had no idea where, but he did know that a password could unlock a door—at least, this is what the ancient tales said. All right then! What if . . .

Anthony shook his head to clear it of the dangerous

ideas that were floating around inside. "I won't go into that room," he said through gritted teeth. "Besides, the chest is gone."

Wearily, Anthony stripped off his clothes and put on his pajamas. He yawned, blew out his candle, stretched, and threw himself into bed. But he lay there wide-eyed, listening to the rumbling of the storm that was getting closer. With a sudden jerk, Anthony hauled himself to his feet and fumbled for the matchbox on the windowsill. With trembling hands he tried to light the candle, but it took him three matches to do it. Then, with the candleholder gripped tightly in his fist, he padded out into the hall and moved stealthily toward the room that had once held the mysterious chest. The door was closed, and it took Anthony a long time to get up the courage to grip the knob. Finally he did, and with a sudden lunge he pushed the door inward. Then he gasped. By the trembling yellow light of the candle, he saw that the chest was there. Had it come because he wanted it to?

Slowly Anthony moved to the side of the chest and knelt down. He pushed the lid up and propped it open with the piece of wood that he had found on the windowsill. Holding the candle down inside the chest, he saw nothing but raw splintery wood. Gripping the edge of the chest with his hands, he stared and stared, but the chest did not change. Now, as he knelt there, Anthony began to feel the horrible urging that he had felt before: *Climb in. Lie down.* For a long time he resisted, while thunder rumbled outside and rain rattled on the window. Finally he clambered over the side of the huge chest and knelt on the bottom. From his shirt pocket he took the card he had found in the vase, and by candlelight he read aloud: *"Auro est locus in quo conflatur."*

At first nothing happened. Then, with a sudden rush of wind, the bottom dropped out of the chest, and Anthony fell downward into darkness.

CHAPTER FOUR

For a terrifying minute Anthony plummeted into the dark. Then his speed slowed and he was floating, until at last he landed gently on a hard surface. Blackness still surrounded him, so he had no idea where he was. Then he reached out and touched rough, splintery wood. He was still inside the chest! Reaching up he pushed at the lid, and with a groaning of rusty hinges it swung open. Anthony gasped—he was not in the dusty room any longer. The chest stood at the edge of a grove of enormous trees. Off to the right loomed a huge mansion of black stone. Gargoyles and other strange decorations sprouted from its clifflike sides. The windows were narrow and set deep into the walls, and thick tangles of bush and weed hid the foundations. The mansion was topped by a steep slate roof with round dormer windows set into it. Anthony could see tall shadowy chimneys capped by elaborate iron covers that reminded him of Chinese pagodas. Near the mansion was a large garden full of twisted weeds and vines, and statues stood here and there amid the growths. A strange shining wall of mist hung at the far end of the garden, and from it came the faint moonlight that lay over this odd night-time world.

Fear gripped Anthony's heart. Where—on or off the earth—was he? One light burned in a second story window of the mansion, so maybe there was someone here who could help him. But the old house looked so gloomy and forbidding that Anthony was not in any hurry to meet the owner. Carefully he raised himself up and stepped over the side of the chest. The ground was covered by soft, springy beds of gray moss, and Anthony made no noise as he padded toward the mansion. Passing the edge of the garden, he heard a dry, rustling sound. He stopped dead in his tracks and stared toward a dark snarl of vines that were writhing and twisting like a mass of snakes. The vines lay still again, and for some reason Anthony felt very relieved. On he plodded, till he came to a winding flagstone path that led up to a low arched doorway set into the side of the house. But when he got nearer Anthony groaned in disappointment. The doorway was a fake! The elaborately carved arch was blocked by a heavy blank slab of stone.

For a long time Anthony stood there with his arms

folded, staring at the false door. He glanced around and examined the leering monster faces and flowers that were carved on the veined marble. Next to the door stood a headless statue of a woman in a toga. She held a cup in one hand, and it was full of black dirt. Near her shoulder a gas bracket sprouted from the dark stone wall. Anthony knew about gas brackets—he had read about them in books. Before the electric light was invented, people's homes were lit by gas, the same kind of gas that is used in stoves and ovens today. In order to get the gas in the pipe to come on, you had to pull on a chain with a ring on the end and light the gas with a candle or a match. Sure enough, there was the chain dangling from the bronze neck of the bracket. *What if I pull at it?* thought Anthony. *What do you think will happen?* Anthony was deathly afraid of escaping gas, and every night before he went to bed he checked the burners on the range in his family's kitchen to make sure that everything was shut off. But out here in the open, gas might escape, and yet nothing bad would happen. Fumbling in his pocket, Anthony brought out a book of matches. He reached up past the shoulder of the statue and pulled at the ring on the end of the chain. Then he quickly opened the matchbook and ripped out a paper match, but he never got the chance to light it. With a deep grinding sound, the heavy stone slab swung inward, revealing a dark shadowy passageway.

Anthony was stunned. He stood staring with his mouth open in utter, total amazement. He had never seen a secret passageway, except in old movies on television. Well, here was one, waiting for him to enter it. But should he go in? As he stood pondering, a greenish flame popped out of the nozzle of the gas bracket and began to dance in the breeze, casting a faint flickering light. Anthony laughed—he didn't know why, but he did. And, for some reason, he felt less afraid. After taking a deep breath and clenching his fists, he plunged into the gaping blackness.

As he stumbled on, feeling his way cautiously, Anthony smelled raw wood, plaster, and dust. The passageway was narrow and wound on in total darkness until Anthony saw a thin shaft of light that fell across the carpeted path on which he was treading. He noticed that the light was coming from a little peephole that was about the size of a half-dollar. Bending over, Anthony peered through the hole and saw an elaborately furnished room. A thick red Oriental carpet lay on the floor, and fancy old-fashioned couches upholstered in red velvet stood near polished Victorian tables and marble busts perched on tall fluted columns. On the walls were dusky paintings in heavy gilt frames, and a strange hovering light filled the room, though Anthony could not figure out where it was coming from. A paneled door was set in the far wall, and at any minute Anthony expected someone to come through it, but no one did.

After peering through the peephole for a few minutes, Anthony moved on. The carpeted floor squeaked under his feet as he tiptoed along, and every noise seemed loud, but no one rushed in to grab him, so he kept going. After several twists and turns, the passage led past three or four more peepholes, but they also peered into empty rooms. On Anthony crept till he came to an opening that seemed a bit larger than the others. It was set very low in the wall, so he had to kneel down to see through it. What Anthony saw made him clamp his hand over his mouth so that his excited gasps would not attract the attention of the people in the room.

Through the tiny opening Anthony saw a strange and frightening scene. In a room that was as richly furnished as any of the others, a meeting was taking place. Grouped around a long polished table were twelve elderly men and women. They all wore black robes, and they looked like creatures from a bad dream. The faces of some of them were sagging and rubbery, as if they were wearing Halloween masks. Other faces were extremely wrinkled and pitted and had eyes that stared weirdly out of deep hollows. At the head of the table sat a tall, gaunt old man with arched black eyebrows. A long mane of white hair hung to his shoulders, and he wore half-moon glasses on his long, ridged nose. His red-rimmed eyes were cold and cruel, and he looked like some evil bird of prey. A jeweled gold star shone on the black velvet robe—it looked like some important military medal from the past or the star of some secret order. Clearly this was the leader of the group, and he spoke in a harsh, grating voice as Anthony listened.

". . . and so, my dear friends, we must find the Logos Cube. It is the key to the world we have built here, and without it this house and the garden outside and the forest and everything would dissolve into mist. It has got to be here somewhere, or we would not be alive. The traitor Nathaniel has hidden it, because he cannot possibly destroy it. And I have an odd feeling that it is very near us—under the floorboards of a room, perhaps, or in a cubbyhole in the attic. We must have it if we are to finish our grand design, our plan."

"But why not leave well enough alone?" wailed a small wizened old woman. "We are all here, and the mansion stands. Perhaps we should abandon our plan and settle for what we have."

The leader glared contemptuously at the woman. "That would be the cowardly way," he said, shaking his head. "No great work was ever done by people who just wanted to hang onto their little plot of ground. Besides, the Logos Cube needs to be controlled—by us. Even though we made it, there are many things about the cube that we do not understand. It has a life of its own, and that life goes on in some hiding place of this enchanted world. The other night, as I lay asleep, I felt the whole mansion tremble, from its chimneys to its foundations. Why did this happen? At another time I was walking along a hallway, and I noticed that a painting that hung on the wall had changed: It had been a landscape, but now it showed a stormy scene at sea. We are walking on brittle ice, my comrades."

"Do you mean that we are going to be destroyed?"

quavered a very frail little man at the far end of the table.

"No," snapped the leader. "I do not think that is likely. But if our world here can change without our permission, then we are in trouble. It might change into something unrecognizable, some world where we would not be happy. That is one good reason why we have to locate the cube."

"But how are we going to do that?" asked the woman who had spoken before. "We don't have a clue, do we?"

The leader smiled unpleasantly. "We have a very small and mysterious clue," he said, drumming his bony fingers on the tabletop. "After the cube was stolen, someone—Nathaniel, probably—carved a Latin phrase on a rock in the garden. As you may recall, it says *Auro est locus in quo conflatur.* There is a place for gold where it is gathered together. Now, this may or may not mean something. If Nathaniel is playing little riddle games with us, the phrase may mean that he has hidden some golden object somewhere, an object that is a clue leading to the discovery of the cube. I will admit that this phrase is not much to go on, but it is all we have."

There was a brief silence. Anthony could hear a gloomy black marble clock ticking on the mantelpiece. Then another old man spoke up. His face was withered and yellowish, and he wore large jeweled rings on his knobby fingers.

"My lord, Great Autarch," he began gravely, "do you think that the traitor Nathaniel still lives?"

The leader cocked his head to one side. Again he grinned, and his yellowish uneven teeth showed. "I suspect that he is still around," he said sourly. "Perhaps he is hiding in the forest or in the old hunting lodge on the far side of Ghost Lake. As you know, it is hard to kill an Autarch, and they can survive for a long time without food." Slowly the leader's face twisted into a mask of bitter hatred. "I wish I had guessed his plan in time," he said angrily, through clenched teeth. "He had doubts about our work from the beginning, and that should have convinced me that he was not to be trusted. If I ever catch him, he will wish that he had not been born."

On and on went this strange conference, while Anthony crouched by the peephole, listening breathlessly. What on earth was going on? What was this place? Who were these people, and what was their grand design? And what could the Logos Cube be? These questions went whirling around in Anthony's head, but he didn't have any answers. And now, as the speakers droned on, Anthony began to be afraid. What if he got caught? Slowly he turned himself around in the narrow passageway and began crawling along the uneven carpeted floor. Around one turn he went, and around another, as the voices faded into the background. Finally Anthony was back at the stone door, which still stood ajar. With a sigh of relief, he stepped out into the chilly night air. He had gotten away! Quickly Anthony glanced around. He half expected to see dark shapes rushing at him from behind bushes and trees. But no one came. Cautiously

Anthony began to move over the mossy ground. He noticed that the murky light had gotten brighter. What did this mean? Nothing, probably. He walked past the edge of the strange overgrown garden and began to hear rustling noises. Looking fearfully to his right, Anthony saw that the tangled vines were writhing and squirming again. And an awful high-pitched wailing sound began. Louder and louder it grew, and to his horror Anthony saw figures running toward him from the shadows near the mansion.

For an instant Anthony stood rooted to the spot, and then he ran. Faster and faster, feet slapping the ground, he pelted on till he reached the chest, which still stood at the edge of the forest. The wailing went on, and Anthony heard harsh barking shouts. By now Anthony was scared half out of his mind, and his fingers fumbled madly with the rough splintery lid. It seemed to take forever, but he finally got it open, and he clambered awkwardly inside. What was the phrase? What was the phrase? Running footsteps pounded closer as Anthony racked his brain. He had just heard the phrase a second or two ago. It was . . . it was . . .

At last it came: *Auro est locus in quo conflatur.* He shouted it loudly into the night and ducked as the heavy lid came slamming down. Once more the bottom dropped out of the chest, and the wild sickening fall to safety began.

CHAPTER FIVE

When Anthony climbed out of the chest again he was in the dark, empty bedroom in the large, creaky old cottage. Rain still rattled on the window, and thunder rumbled endlessly. With shaking hands Anthony lowered the lid of the chest and stumbled out into the hall. Lightning rushed back and forth over the warped boards, and it lit the stern faces of the people who stared down from their gilded frames on the wall. Anthony felt dizzy and sick to his stomach, like someone who has been thrown into a giant Mixmaster. *What had he seen?* Blearily he looked around, and he felt a tremendous desire to sleep. He could hardly keep his eyes open, but somehow he dragged himself down the hall to his bedroom.

With an exhausted sigh, he heaved himself onto the bed and was asleep in a few seconds.

Days passed. Miss Eells and Emerson noticed that a change had come over Anthony, and it worried them. He didn't say much, and his mind always seemed to be somewhere else. At mealtime the two older people would ask him questions, but all they got were one-word answers. Sometimes in the evening, when Emerson and Miss Eells came in from fishing, they would find Anthony sitting silently on the porch of the cottage, listening to music on the radio. All this strange hermitlike behavior was scary, and it began to look as if Anthony was suffering from some form of mental illness. Miss Eells was beginning to get panicky, but as usual Emerson remained calm. He was determined to get to the bottom of the whole business, and he didn't believe that Anthony was losing his mind. Something else was bothering him, and Emerson wanted to know what it was.

One evening after dinner, Emerson walked out to the end of the dock and sat down next to Anthony, who was squatting cross-legged and looking out at the far end of the lake, where a dusky crimson sun was setting in a mass of dark blue clouds. The look on Anthony's face was faraway and dreamy, as if he was living in some other world. After a quick, anxious glance at him, Emerson lowered himself down onto the dock and put his hand on Anthony's arm.

"My boy," he began quietly, "my sister and I are

worried about you. You don't . . . well, you just don't seem to be yourself these days. Is something wrong?"

No answer. Anthony went on staring straight ahead.

Emerson paused. He took his pocket watch out of his vest pocket, popped the lid, squinted at the time, and put the watch back. "Anthony," he began brusquely, "I did not come down here to sit and stare at the sunset with you. If you are unhappy about this vacation trip, please tell us and we'll take you home. But this moping has become intolerable, and it has to stop!"

Anthony stiffened. A shudder passed through his body. Then, sobbing brokenly, he turned to Emerson and threw his arms around him. "I . . . I've got . . . something to . . . to tell you," said Anthony in a thick, weepy voice. "But you . . . you have to believe me . . . you . . . really do."

Emerson nodded solemnly as he hugged his weeping friend. "I'll believe you," he said, "because I know you're honest, and besides, it's pretty clear that you have been through an awful experience of some kind. Tell me all about it."

When he finally had control of himself again, Anthony told Emerson his amazing tale. About the appearing and disappearing chest and the strange otherworld that he had been thrust into. When he was through, Anthony looked at Emerson to see what his reaction was. He was terribly afraid that Emerson would be amused, but Emerson wasn't laughing. He looked awestruck.

"Good God!" he exclaimed softly, as he stared out at the setting sun. "I have heard of such things, but I did not think they were possible—not until now, that is."

Anthony stared hard at Emerson. "Do . . . do you know what happened to me?" he asked in a faltering voice. "Do you know where that mansion is?"

Emerson smiled wryly. "The mansion is a long, long way from here, my friend. A *long* way." Emerson paused and picked up a flat pebble that lay on the slats of the dock. With a flick of his wrist he sent the pebble skipping across the still waters of the lake. "I think," he went on gravely, "that you were projected into another dimension. Into a world that does not exist anywhere on this earth. It's not in outer space either. It's . . . well, I just have to say it's in another dimension. You see, Anthony, for a long time people have wondered if there were any other worlds like ours existing on different planes . . . you know, sort of like on different floors of an apartment house. In your case, you seem to have stumbled upon a world that is held in place by magic. These weird creatures whose conference you eavesdropped on, they are the ones who built the world—they're sort of like the folks who put together a model train layout, though a good deal more clever. I think that those black-robed characters once lived in our world. But they didn't like it very much, so they moved next door, so to speak. But there is a connecting tunnel—that chest that doesn't seem able to stay put. Now, as for this thing called the Logos Cube . . . well, I can only guess that it's the heart of the world our black-robed friends created. And from what you said, it seems to have been swiped by someone. Beyond that, I'm just as much in the dark as you are. But this talk about a grand design bothers me. What do you suppose those creeps are up to?"

Anthony shrugged. "Your guess is as good as mine, Mr. Eells. I'm just glad you believe me."

"Oh, I believe you—I really do," murmured Emerson, as he gazed thoughtfully out across the darkening lake. "In fact, I believe you so much that I'd like to go have a look at this mansion myself."

Anthony's mouth dropped open. "What did you say?"

Emerson calmly flicked a piece of lint off his shirt. "I *said*, I'd like to take a look at the place myself. I mean, it isn't every day that you get a chance to visit another world. Besides, if those characters are up to something, I'd like to know what it is."

Anthony was flabbergasted. Here was Emerson talking about visiting the strange and frightening world of the mansion, and he was talking calmly! He might have been getting ready to go visit his cousin Hattie in Bemidji, or something like that.

Anthony's mouth opened and closed, but no sound came out. Finally he found his voice. "Mr. Eells!" he gasped. "Aren't you scared?"

Emerson gave Anthony an odd look. "Of course I am. But scientific curiosity overcomes my fear—I just want to see what that place looks like!"

Later that evening, as the three of them sat playing cards in the lamplit parlor of the cottage, Emerson and Anthony talked about the chest to Miss Eells. She was very relieved to know that Anthony was not losing his mind, but she was thoroughly alarmed at the idea that Emerson was planning to go and spy on those evil black-robed plotters.

"Em, are you out of your mind?" exclaimed Miss Eells as she pitched a card onto the table. "They almost caught Anthony, and they might catch you. You might be tortured or killed or . . . or *anything!*"

"Oh, I don't know about that," said Emerson calmly. "I have ways of protecting myself. By the way, Myra, you can't play a heart till hearts have been broken."

Miss Eells snatched the card back and threw out a spade. "Don't try to change the subject, Em. What on earth do you mean by protection?"

Emerson grinned. "I mean my amulet collection. Surely there's something in there that will help."

Anthony's mouth dropped open. He knew what Emerson was talking about: Emerson was a lawyer by profession, but his hobby was magic. The study of his home in St. Cloud was crammed with books on magic and the occult, and on the shelves and the library table were cases containing objects that were supposed to be magic. Emerson had brought some of them with him to the cottage, in a mahogany case that had once held silverware. Many times in the last two weeks Anthony had seen Emerson with the case open in his lap. He was poring over his treasures, peering at them through a magnifying glass. The amulets were indeed an odd collection: There was a glass tube full of sand from the Gobi desert—it had been blessed by a Tibetan monk. There was a medieval German coin hanging from a chain of bronze links. A flat glass case containing a scrap of paper that had been found on the body of a bishop after he died. Turkish coins with mystical inscriptions on them, miniature Russian icons in gold frames, cloth scapulars with pictures of obscure saints on them. Gold-mounted teeth from the skulls of long-dead wizards, and brass medals and tiny ivory statuettes that glowed in the dark. All the amulets were fitted with chains or stout leather straps so that they could be worn to ward off evil.

After an awkward silence, Miss Eells spoke up. She was just as skeptical as ever, besides being angry and frightened. "Look here, Em," she began in a severe tone, "do you really think these trinkets will keep you from being grabbed by those weird-looking nuts in the mansion? Good heavens, you've never tested these things! For all you know, they wouldn't ward off a gnat! And here you are, ready to risk your life with this kind of idiotic protection. It's insane, Em, utterly and totally insane!"

"You may think so, Myra," said Emerson frostily, "but I am of another opinion. All of these amulets came to me with documents that proved their reliability—at least, they proved it to me. I know, I know . . . documents sometimes lie. But these are signed by famous sorcerers, and I'm inclined to believe them. So if I were you, I wouldn't order my coffin yet—I'll be out there and back in a jiffy!"

"Famous last words," muttered Miss Eells. "So when are you going?"

Emerson coughed nervously and glanced away. "Uh, well . . . there's a slight problem. The chest isn't in the room. And I don't really know when it'll be back."

Miss Eells threw back her head and laughed—she just couldn't help it.

Emerson's face was beginning to get red—he hated to be made fun of. "I'm sure the chest will be in the room sometime soon," he said in a stiff, formal voice. "Magical things do not follow regular schedules like railway trains. We will simply have to check the room from time to time. Now, as I recall, it is Anthony's turn to play a card. Let's get on with the game."

More days passed. Wild evening storms came up out of nowhere, and thunder rattled the windows of the rambling old cottage. The three vacationers followed their aimless schedule of fishing, card playing, eating, and just sitting around doing nothing, but every now and then they would check the mysterious back room that smelled strongly of dust. Unfortunately, the chest was never there. Anthony began to wonder if it was gone forever, and—to tell the truth—he really hoped it was. He didn't believe that Emerson could go and spy on those evil creatures and get away. He would meet with an awful end, and Anthony himself would feel responsible, because he had discovered the secret password that activated the old chest. For the time being, however, it was pretty clear that no one was going anywhere—no chest, no trip. It was as simple as that.

One chilly evening the three vacationers came rowing home after a successful time fishing out on the lake. A red sun was setting behind the distant pine trees, and its bloody light stained the ripply waters. Emerson had caught three lovely striped bass, and they lay in the wicker creel in the bottom of the rowboat. With one last pull Emerson sent the boat gliding in next to the dock. But as he was reaching out to tie the mooring rope up to one of the posts, he let out a loud exclamation.

"My Lord! For the love of God, would you get a load of that!"

Anthony and Miss Eells looked where Emerson was pointing. In a second-story window of the cottage a lamp was burning. With a lump in his throat, Anthony realized that this was the window of the room where he had found the chest. But all the oil lamps were downstairs—they always were. When they went to bed Anthony and the others took candles from a collection that lay on a table at the foot of the stairs. So why was there a light in that upper room?

Emerson looked at Miss Eells, and Miss Eells looked at Anthony. Everyone was thinking the same thing, and so as quickly as possible they tied the boat up to the dock and clattered down the boards to the front door of the cottage. Abruptly, Emerson shoved the creel full of fish into Anthony's arms and told him to take them to the icehouse. Then, at breakneck speed Emerson tore into the house and up the stairs. A moment later Miss Eells and Anthony heard bellowing down the stairs.

"It's here! The chest is here! I don't believe it, but it really truly is here! Lord have mercy on us!"

Miss Eells gasped. What on earth was going to happen now? Anthony still stood there in the front hall with the dripping creel in his arms. Like Miss Eells, he was wondering, what next? Oh, well, first things first, he said to himself glumly, and he went around to the side of the house to put the fish in the cooler. When Anthony got back to the front door of the house, he found Emerson standing in the hall with an excited look on his face. Actually Emerson was more than excited—he was bubbling with awe and wonder and fear. Anthony had never seen him in such a state. Usually Emerson was the calm, cool, and collected type. He gave you the feeling that he could handle just about any situation, however wild and bizarre it might be. But right now Emerson was a mess.

"It's true! It's really true!" he babbled, looking wildly this way and that. "Anthony, I will admit that I doubted your story for a little instant or two—or maybe even three. But now I've seen the blasted thing with my own eyes! A gateway to another world!"

"It's the gateway to Hell," said Miss Eells grimly.

"And if you go through it, Em, you're an even bigger fool than I think you are!"

This remark really stung Emerson, and he flinched. But then he pulled himself together and squared his shoulders. "I'm going," he announced stubbornly, "and that's all there is to it!" He turned to Anthony. "Anthony, my boy," he said, "will you go with me? I need you to guide me. With amulets around our necks, we'll be perfectly safe, I promise you."

At this Miss Eells completely lost her temper. "Emerson Eells!" she exclaimed furiously. "Are you so irresponsible that you would lead this young man into terrible danger? You ought to be ashamed of yourself!"

Emerson blushed and stared at the floor. "You don't have to come if you don't want to, Anthony," he said in a low voice.

Strangely enough, Anthony found that he was eager to go. He was scared, of course, but he also wanted to revisit that strange, shadowy world. After a short pause he spoke up. "I'll go, Mr. Eells," he said firmly. "When do we start?"

"Now. I'll get the amulets," Emerson said. For himself he chose the tube of sand from the Gobi desert. Anthony picked a miniature Russian icon of St. Basil the Great, and together they climbed the creaky stairs of the old cottage and walked down the hall toward the room where the chest was. After a deep sigh Miss Eells went to the living room and lit three of the oil lamps. Then she sat down in a rocking chair and grimly went to work on her knitting. She was trying to make a sweater for her niece's small daughter, and it was not coming out very well—one arm was longer than the other, and the stitches kept coming unraveled. But it was all she could think of to do at this point. The rocker creaked, the knitting needles clacked, and the Waterbury clock on the shelf ticked noisily. Miss Eells heard the lid of the chest slam loudly, and she jumped. *God help us now*, she thought. *God help us all now*.

CHAPTER SIX

The night dragged on, and still Emerson and Anthony did not return. Miss Eells threw her knitting into a corner and paced up and down the living room floor, chewing her lip anxiously. Every now and then she would go to the front door of the cottage, open it, and peer out into the night. The wind was rising, and it made an eerie sound among the thick-clustered pines. After staring into the pitch-blackness for a while, Miss Eells would close the door and go on pacing while the shelf clock ticked endlessly. Miss Eells was a good imaginer, and she was dreaming up all sorts of horrible things that might have happened. Finally, at a little after two in the morning, the chest lid slammed thunderously overhead. Oh, thank God! breathed Miss Eells, as she clasped her hands prayerfully. Presently she heard footsteps on the squeaky steps, and she rushed to the bottom of the staircase. Out of the shadows Emerson and Anthony appeared. They both looked pale and haggard, and sweat was streaming down their faces. Woodenly they clumped on down, and Miss Eells stepped out of the way to let them pass. She followed them into the living room and watched as they sagged into armchairs. So far, neither one of them had said a word.

Miss Eells perched on a rocking chair and waited. Finally Emerson spoke. He sounded incredibly weary, and his voice shook.

"I never would have believed that it was possible," he said, as he took off his glasses and cleaned them with his handkerchief. "I really never would have! But it's true! That strange otherworldly world is really out there, and I'll tell you something else. The world is in danger—our world, I mean. I don't want to sound over-dramatic, but we've got to do something, and we've got to do it soon!"

Miss Eells looked utterly bewildered. "Em, what on earth do you mean?" she asked. "You are talking absolute total nonsense!"

Emerson stared hard at his sister, and a weary frown curled his lips. "Am I? Am I really?" With a heavy sigh, he picked up his meerschaum pipe, which lay in a glass ashtray on a nearby table. He unzipped a leather pouch and filled the pipe. Then he struck a match. Clouds of smoke spewed out into the room. "Tell her,

Anthony," Emerson sighed. "Tell her the whole ghastly, unlikely story."

Anthony's mouth dropped open. He had never thought that he was terribly good with words, and here was Emerson asking him to tell the tale! Anthony took a deep breath, and after a lot of hemming and hawing he began: They had wound up spying on another meeting of the Autarchs, and they really got an earful. The Autarchs and their servants were turning the mansion and the grounds upside down looking for the mysterious Logos Cube. As Anthony had heard before, they needed it to keep their otherdimensional world in place. But they had another purpose, a far more sinister one in mind. They wanted to use the cube to drag the earth and its inhabitants off into their dimension.

Anthony stopped talking, and for a long time no one said anything. The clock clattered on, and the wind rattled the windows of the old cottage. Finally Miss Eells spoke.

"It all seems a bit hard to believe," she said in a weak, throaty voice. "I mean . . ."

"Yes, it is hard to believe," snapped Emerson, cutting in suddenly. "But then appearing and disappearing chests are hard to believe too. Mansions in other dimensions are hard to believe. But those things are there— Anthony and I have seen them. Maybe it's impossible for the Autarchs to find the Logos Cube. Maybe it's impossible for them to carry out their nasty, unthinkable scheme. But what if they could do it? Would you enjoy living in a world lit by misty moonlight, a world where plants scream and vines try to grab you? No, I didn't think you would. And I'll tell you something else. In case you think that the Autarchs would be kindly dictators, I've found out what happened to the three people I rented this cottage to a few years ago."

Miss Eells's jaw dropped. "You have?"

Emerson nodded grimly. "Yes. As Anthony and I were leaving the mansion, I happened to glance toward that evil garden. It has three statues in it, three very strange statues in the shape of people writhing in hideous torment. The light was weak, but it was good enough for me to see the face of one of the figures, and . . ." Emerson paused and swallowed hard. ". . . and," he went on in a strained voice, ". . . and the face looked very much like the face of one of the three tourists who rented this cottage from me."

Miss Eells stared in amazement. "You mean . . ." she began hesitantly. "You mean . . ."

"Yes, I do indeed mean," said Emerson. "Somehow those three poor people discovered the secret of the chest. They probably used the card that Anthony found in that dusty old vase, and they paid for their curiosity with their lives. It's awful to think about, isn't it? And that is the fate that lies in store for people in our world if they come under the domination of the Autarchs."

"I don't think they can do it," muttered Anthony stubbonly. "They're not powerful enough to do that, are they? Well, are they?"

Emerson heaved a weary sigh. "I don't know," he said slowly. "I honestly do not know. But as long as there is even a small chance that such an evil thing might happen, I think I had better go back there and find that dratted cube."

Miss Eells was aghast. "Em, have you gone completely out of your mind? You haven't a clue that would lead you to the cube."

Emerson stared at the burning tobacco in the bowl of his pipe. "Oh, I don't know about that," he said. "There is that card that Anthony found. Where is it, by the way?"

Anthony got up and walked across the room to a round mahogany end table. He yanked open a drawer and pulled out a wrinkled piece of cardboard. Without a word he handed it to Emerson, who adjusted his glasses and squinted at the neat square printing.

"*Auro est locus in quo conflatur,*" he muttered. "Gold, gathered together somewhere. A nugget? A gold statuette? A necklace? And how would such a thing help us find the Logos Cube? I can't imagine how. Then there's this thing about the great clue being in the Temple of the Winds. But I didn't see anything that looked like a miniature temple when we were at the mansion. Of course, there may be more to that ghoulish estate than what we've seen. There's that mass of trees, and who knows what may lie beyond it? At any rate, I intend to go back and explore, and I will not listen to anyone who tells me not to go!" Emerson folded his arms and looked as stubborn as he possibly could.

Miss Eells was near despair. "Well, if you want to kill yourself, I suppose it's your own business," she said bitterly.

"Oh, I don't know," said Emerson, who was turning back into his usual optimistic self. "I got the two of us back safe and sound, didn't I?"

Miss Eells said nothing for several minutes. Then she pulled herself to her feet and yawned. "I don't know about you two, but I'm going to bed. And if I were you, Emerson Eells, I'd think long and hard before I went back to that dark and dangerous place. You may think you're saving the world, but you'll end up breaking your neck!"

Emerson sniffed disdainfully. Then he got up and walked off to the foot of the stairs to get a candle to light his way to bed. The other two followed him.

CHAPTER SEVEN

For the next several days Miss Eells and Anthony tried to go on with their vacation life of fishing and boating, which was a bit hard to do at this point. Emerson went with them sometimes, but it was clear that his mind was someplace else. Many times during the day he would go up to the room where the chest appeared, and he would stand in the doorway chewing his lip impatiently and drumming his fingers on the woodwork. "There has got to be a reason why the chest shows up when it does," Emerson would mutter from time to time. "It can't just be chance." He examined every inch of the barren, dusty little room, but he found only one odd thing: The window was divided into nine small panes, and the one in the upper right-hand corner had turned purple. This usually happens only in very old houses with glass that is 200 years old or more. Impurities in the glass mix with sunlight to cause this change, but—as Emerson said to himself—this cottage was only about ninety years old. Which meant that somebody had deliberately put that purple pane up there. But why?

One evening as the three vacationers were enjoying a delicious fish dinner in the kitchen, Emerson announced that he had figured it all out. He had a very irritating know-it-all way of telling people about his discoveries, but Anthony and Miss Eells were used to him by now.

"The chest appears when some star or other shines through that purple pane," he said, as he munched a piece of fish. "That has got to be the explanation." Fussily, Emerson plucked a bone out of his fish fillet and laid it on the edge of his plate.

Miss Eells eyed her brother skeptically. "Then why doesn't the stupid chest appear every night? The summer constellations are in the sky now, and they'll be there for quite a while. If some star controls that chest, it would have been shining in the window at the same time every night for at least several weeks."

"Not if the sky was overcast," said Emerson smugly. "Personally, I think the star must be Arcturus. It is in the southern sky at present, and that window faces south."

"But wouldn't the chest disappear when the star moved past the window, or when clouds came to cover the stars?" put in Anthony timidly. He never felt good about challenging Emerson's theories, but in this case he felt he had to.

Emerson rubbed his chin and looked thoughtful. "Good comment," he muttered. "Very good. As I recall, your solo expedition took place during a storm. But the stars had been out earlier that night, before the storm arose. All I can say is this: The star must make the chest appear, and once it's there, the chest stays until morning and then vanishes. Does that sound reasonable to you?"

"About as reasonable as pineapple upside-down cake," said Miss Eells tartly. "As *I* recall, the very first time Anthony saw the chest, the stars were out, all right. But he took us straight up to the room, and the chest had disappeared. How do you explain that, Emerson Einstein Eells?"

Emerson looked cranky, but then he chuckled. "Elementary, my dear Myra. Anthony said he opened the chest and then closed it again. Obviously, opening the chest prepares it for its journey to Whatsis Land. We know what a *person* then has to do to travel in the chest: Climb in and say the magic words. But suppose you *didn't* want to make the trip yourself?"

Miss Eells muttered, "That wouldn't strain my supposer at all."

Emerson ignored her. "Let's say you only wanted to send some *object* to Foggy Bottom, something like, oh, a CARE package or an A-bomb. An object couldn't say the magical abracadabra, so you'd simply put it inside the chest and close the lid. Closing the lid puts the contraption on automatic pilot and sends it on its merry way. So when Anthony closed the thing, he dispatched it to the other dimension. By the time we got to the room, the chest was off to the land of mist."

Miss Eells snorted. "You have an answer for everything, don't you, Mr. Smarty? I suppose we have to wait for a clear night to see if your theory works. Personally, I hope the sky stays clouded over till Labor Day. I think you're crazy to want to go back to that mansion!"

Emerson said nothing, but he got up and went to the cookstove to see if there were any fish fillets left. He had caught the fish himself, so of course he thought they tasted delicious.

Three straight days of rain and cloudy weather followed. All day it drizzled, and at night heavy downpours hid the lake from sight. Finally, though, the weather cleared, and Emerson began to get all worked up. It was a Thursday in mid-July, and that night he would be going back. Meanwhile, Miss Eells and Anthony had done a lot of talking in secret, and they had finally reached a decision: Come hell or high water they would go with Emerson. Anthony was sure he could help Emerson in some way, and Miss Eells felt that she would go out of her mind waiting for the other two to return. Besides, she was beginning to believe in the power of the amulets.

When Miss Eells and Anthony told Emerson about their decision, he nearly had a fit.

"Nonsense!" he exclaimed, folding his arms indignantly. "It's far too dangerous! I won't hear of it!"

"I thought you told us that anyone wearing one of your amulets would be safe," said Miss Eells with a malicious gleam in her eye.

Emerson got flustered. His face turned red and he began to splutter. "Well, I . . . that is, I . . . oh, blast it all, I'll tell you the truth! I said that to keep you from worrying. The place is as dangerous as a quicksand bog. But someone has to go to find the clue that may lead to the Logos Cube. When I let Anthony go with me last time, it was because I felt lonely and afraid. But since then I've regretted that decision, and now I say to you both: *Stay home!*"

Miss Eells glared at her brother. "Em, dear," she said, "if you want the two of us to stay here you'd better be good at knots and tying people up with clothesline. And remember, while you're working on one of us, the other one will be beating you over the head with a breadboard or a frying pan."

Emerson was feeling desperate. "I . . . I won't let you use my amulets," he said with a pouty frown. "And may I remind you that I have the only key to the storage case?"

Miss Eells grinned. "You think you have the only key. Years ago you gave me a duplicate, because you felt I was levelheaded and wouldn't do anything rash." She reached in under the collar of her blouse and pulled out a small silver key on a beaded chain.

Emerson looked at his two friends. Then he heaved a deep weary sigh and shook his head. "Oh, all *right!*" he said staunchily. "But if one of you gets turned to stone, don't come whining to me about it!"

That evening the three adventurers got ready to go. They put on warm sweaters, because the air of the otherworld was always clammy and cold. Anthony brought a flashlight, and Emerson carried a crowbar, in case there was a door that had to be forced. Once again Emerson wore the tube of Gobi desert sand, and Anthony used the tiny Russian icon. Miss Eells picked a Joachimsthaler, a huge German coin from the sixteenth century. It hung from a handsome braided gold chain and had been blessed by the Bishop of Cologne. Stepping out onto the porch of the cottage, Emerson saw that the sky was clear and clustered thick with stars. Arcturus burned clearly in the south.

"Here goes nothing," whispered Emerson to himself, and he stepped back inside the house. The other two were waiting at the foot of the stairs, and up they went, single file. When they reached the room at the back there was the chest waiting for them. Emerson walked bravely forward and lifted the heavy lid.

"One at a time," he said in a voice that trembled slightly. "I'll go first, and if I'm not back in five minutes, I'll send the empty chest for you, and that will mean that it's nighttime in Ghastlyland and that you can follow me. Okay?"

Miss Eells and Anthony nodded. They both swallowed hard and watched anxiously as Emerson stepped into the chest, squatted down, and pulled the lid shut. His muttered words could hardly be heard, but after a short pause the chest shimmered and vanished. Miss Eells turned to Anthony. A thought had just occurred to her.

"Anthony?" she asked. "How do you get the chest to come back here empty?"

Anthony grinned. "Mr. Eells figured that out the night the two of us went together. You stand in the chest and say the words, and then you get out real quick and shut the lid. It's kind of tricky, but it works."

Miss Eells gave Anthony a sidelong glance. "I must be nuts to be doing this," she said to herself. "But then, I've known for years that I was off my rocker. Oh, well. At my age, I haven't long to live anyway."

After this cheerful remark, Miss Eells fell silent. The two of them waited in the empty room for what seemed like ages. Then, with a slight whispering sound, the chest reappeared. Anthony and Miss Eells looked at each other. Neither of them wanted to go, but they knew they had to. Finally Anthony took a deep breath and stepped forward. He opened the lid and climbed in.

"I'll . . . I'll send it back for you, Miss Eells," he said in a high-pitched nervous voice. "It . . . it won't take long." And with that Anthony squatted down, closed the lid, and muttered the magic formula. Again a pause, then a shimmer in the air, and the chest vanished once more. Miss Eells chewed her lip and paced up and down. In a few minutes the chest came back for her.

"I feel like a paratrooper getting ready for his first jump," she said to herself as she climbed into the chest. It took a while before she got up the courage to kneel down and pull the heavy lid back into place. *Auro est locus in quo conflatur*, she said quietly, and then she closed her eyes tight. In a few seconds the terrifying drop began. Then her fall slowed and she landed with a soft bump. Emerson jerked the lid open and peered in.

"Did you have a nice ride, Myra?" he asked wryly.

Miss Eells gave her brother a dirty look and clambered out of the chest. With an awestruck look on her face, she peered around at the strange, misty moonlit world. She was frightened, but she fought down her fear and grinned weakly. "So where do we go from here, brother?" she asked. "You don't have a map, so it'll have to be done by guesswork. Right?"

Emerson nodded glumly. "Right. Off to the left there is a forest, and I think I see a path. Paths usually lead somewhere, so we'll take it." Emerson glanced quickly over his shoulder. "The windows in the mansion are dark, so let us hope that the Autarchs are in bed. Even sorcerers need their sleep, after all."

In single file, with Emerson in the lead, they entered the dark, shadowy forest. As they trudged along the sandy path, alarming things began to happen. Branches groped at them, and the trees made odd groaning sounds. At one point a vine on the ground reached out and tried to grab Anthony's ankle. But it pulled back suddenly and lay flat.

"I have to hand it to you, Em," whispered Miss Eells. "Those amulets work."

"Of course they work," snapped Emerson. "You don't think I'd lead you into danger without some sort of protection, do you? And now I think we're deep enough into the forest for me to turn on the flashlight. Besides, it's pitch-black in here, and sooner or later one of us is going to slam into a tree trunk."

Emerson clicked on the flashlight, and it burned with a foggy, wavering glow. They tried to ignore the thick-clustered dark trees that seemed to be watching them. Very soon they came out into the open—apparently the trees were just a grove and not a large forest at all. The three adventurers found that they were at the edge of a small lake covered with lily pads and a gray scum. On the other side of the lake stood a small eight-sided building with a columned porch and a copper dome. In the distance was the gleaming wall of mist that hung beyond the garden and the mansion.

"Charming scene, eh?" said Emerson sourly. "If you were a real estate agent you'd go out of your mind trying to sell this place."

Miss Eells looked thoughtful. "Em," she said slowly, "why did the Autarchs make this place such an awful one? I mean, if they can work magic, why didn't they create a pleasant estate with sunshine and normal moonlight and starlight?"

"I suspect that this estate *had* to turn out the way it did," Emerson answered, with a sad shake of his head. "Either the magic went haywire, or . . . well, who knows? You should also remember that the Autarchs were once ordinary people living in our ordinary everyday world. Creating this estate deformed their bodies and their minds. They've probably been here so long now that they don't realize what a monstrous place this is. Love of power has replaced ordinary human feelings in their minds. Of course, from what Anthony heard, there was one rebel who refused to accept the values of the Autarchs, and he's the one who hid the Logos Cube. Anyway, let's stop jawing and follow this path around the edge of the lake. I'll bet any money that little domed building is the Temple of the Winds."

Once more Emerson began to walk along the edge of the small lake, playing the beam of the flashlight before him. A heavy stillness hung over the lake—no crickets, no frogs, no sign of anything living. Soon the three of them were standing before the columned porch of the little building. Sure enough, on the marble cornice above the pillars these words were carved: TEMPLE OF THE WINDS.

A short flight of broad, cracked stone steps led to the porch, and beyond was a bronze door that stood half ajar. Emerson's light continued to burn foggily, because this was an evil and cursed place. But he plunged ahead and shoved at the door, and with a loud groan it scraped inward. Emerson stepped inside and played his light around. And then he almost laughed. The temple was full of gardening equipment! On a warped table stood stacks of clay flowerpots, and a trowel lay nearby. Rakes and hoes leaned against the wall, and there was even an old-fashioned mechanical lawn mower. Hedge clippers and sickles hung from brackets, and overhead was a dark oil lamp on a chain.

"Humph! If this doesn't beat everything!" muttered Emerson. "You know, I'll bet all this stuff belonged to the rebel, the one who split away from the Autarchs. He was probably trying to make this miserable dump a bit more human. But the sixty-four dollar question still is: *Where* is this so-called great clue?"

For a long time Emerson and his friends poked around. They looked under flowerpots and on the sills of the narrow windows. They peered into the blades of the lawn mower and moved rakes and scraped around on their hands and knees in dusty, dirty corners. But they came up empty.

"Phooey on this miserable place anyway!" growled Emerson, as he dragged himself to his feet. "The Autarchs must have searched here, and if they didn't find anything, I don't see how we can expect to." He wiped sweat off his forehead with his sleeve and gazed blearily around. He had been working so hard that he was panting, and he felt thoroughly dejected. Anthony looked gloomy too—he hung his head and felt tears trickling down his cheeks. Only Miss Eells seemed optimistic. She darted her head around and smiled weirdly.

"Oh, I don't know, Em," she said, as she began shifting the objects on the dusty table. "We haven't *completely* ransacked this place. I see that these inner walls are made of brick. Maybe one of them is loose. In the meantime I suggest that we take out our anger on these flowerpots here. I can damage things without trying to, but sometimes it's fun to . . ." Instead of finishing her sentence, Miss Eells picked up a flowerpot and pitched it against a wall. Pieces of red clay flew everywhere. Grinning wickedly, Miss Eells threw another pot and another, while Emerson and Anthony gaped in amazement. But when she heaved the next pot, something unexpected happened: A small shiny object went spinning out of the clay fragments and landed in the middle of the room. With a loud exclamation, Emerson swooped down and picked it up. He played his flashlight's beam over it.

"Heavens!" he breathed. "Do you know what this is? It's a Brasher doubloon!"

Miss Eells and Anthony stared in bewilderment. Emerson might as well have told them that he had found a packet of stardust or the Wizard of Oz's hat. When he saw that the other two were thoroughly befuddled, Emerson sighed and began to explain. Ephraim Brasher was a rich planter in Virginia before the Revolutionary War. A neighbor of George Washington's, in fact. Well, back in those days private citizens could make gold and silver coins. All they needed was the metal and a coin press. Mr. Brasher struck some gold coins called doubloons, and only three are known to exist today. Needless to say, they are priceless and are all in museums or private collections.

"And here is a fourth one," said Emerson, holding the coin up. "But whoever owned it has lowered its value a great deal by scratching a word on one side with a knife." Emerson handed the coin to Anthony, and he peered at it as the pale beam of the flashlight played over it. Sure enough, on one side of the coin the word WABE had been scratched in large capital letters.

Anthony looked bewildered and gave the coin to Miss Eells so she could examine it. After squinting at the carved word, she looked up. "And who or what is a *wabe*?" she asked. "Sounds like baby talk for *wave*, doesn't it?"

Emerson shrugged. "Could be someone's name, or just a piece of incredible folderol. Or a practical joke. But if this is the so-called great clue, I'll take vanilla, thank you." He banged his flashlight on the table and stood staring angrily at the blank wall.

Miss Eells gently patted her brother on the arm. "Look, Em," she said quietly, "the meaning of clues isn't always clear. Maybe if we take the coin back with us and think a while in the peace and quiet of the cottage, we will decipher the meaning of the word. So come on. Let's get out of this awful, cursed place."

Emerson didn't need to be persuaded. With a little shrug he stuck the coin in his pocket and led the way out of the door, down the steps, and along the sandy patch to the grove of trees. None of them liked the idea of entering that gloomy sinister clump of trees again, but they had to. Again the trees groaned and creaked, and vines groped feebly at them. But they were not stopped, and soon they stood by the chest again. One at a time, as before, they went back: Emerson first, then Anthony, and finally Miss Eells. Just before she climbed into the chest, Miss Eells took a quick look around. The mansion was still dark, and the plants and vines in the garden rustled uneasily because an intruder was near. Miss Eells did not notice a dark figure standing in the shadow of the grove of trees.

CHAPTER EIGHT

When the three adventurers got back to the cottage, only an hour and a half had passed, according to their clocks. They all felt incredibly weary and threw themselves into bed without even changing into their pajamas. The next morning, as they sat around the kitchen table eating ham and eggs and drinking coffee and milk, Anthony and his friends felt a bit woozy, and the trip they had taken seemed like an unpleasant dream. But there was the Brasher doubloon shining on the table in front of them. It was real; their otherworldly adventure had been real. When he finished eating, Emerson lit his meerschaum pipe and leaned back in his chair.

"Wabe," he said thoughtfully. "Maybe it's initials for

something like Will All Babies Expectorate."

Anthony looked puzzled: "What does *expectorate*, mean?"

Miss Eells laughed. "It's a polite word for 'spit.' That's a wonderful reading of the clue, Em. I'm sure that's exactly what the word means."

"I was not being serious, Myra. Hmm. Wabe. Wabe. Backward it's Ebaw, but that's not very helpful either. Hmm. Hmm." He went back to puffing on his pipe and thinking. Meanwhile, Anthony cleared the plates off the table and scraped the leftover food into the garbage pail. Miss Eells boiled water on the stove in a huge teakettle, so they would have hot water for doing the dishes. Suddenly Emerson let out a loud roar and banged his fist on the table.

"By God! I have it! How stupid of me not to have seen it before!"

Miss Eells whirled suddenly and with a sweep of her arm knocked a teacup off the drainboard of the sink. "Good heavens, Em!" she exclaimed. "What did you find? The answer to the riddle of the universe?"

Emerson smiled. "Well, not exactly that. But something nearly as good. Do you remember the *Jabberwocky* poem in Lewis Carroll's *Through the Looking Glass*?"

"Yes, of course I do. But I can't recite it from memory."

Emerson looked smug. "Well, I can. It begins like this:

'Twas brillig, and the slithy toves
Did gyre and gimble in the wabe:
All mimsy were the borogoves,
And the mome raths outgrabe.

See? It mentions 'Wabe,' doesn't it? But, you will say, these are nonsense words in a nonsense poem, and they mean nothing. And the answer is, not necessarily. You see, there is a character in the poem—a real know-it-all type, like me—named Humpty Dumpty. And he tries to explain to Alice what the words in *Jabberwocky* mean. The important part is this: He claims that *Wabe* means 'The plot of grass around a sundial.' Well, Humpty may be talking through his hat, but this clue—probably left by the mysterious rebel Autarch—is important. If there's a sundial on that blasted estate, the Logos Cube is probably buried near it. Doesn't that seem likely?"

Miss Eells laughed. "Em, I don't know if you've noticed it, but whenever you come up with some far-fetched explanation, you say something like, 'Well, now, isn't that logical? Isn't that reasonable?' Quite honestly, this *wabe* business seems like pie in the sky. For all you know, the rebel—the guy who left the clue—may be named Cyrus Q. Wabe. Or maybe he scratched that word on there just for the fun of it. Or to throw people off. If this character really did hide the Whatsis Cube, would he have left clues leading to its discovery? Wouldn't he have just destroyed the stupid thing?"

Emerson's face was beginning to get red. "It may not be possible for anyon to destroy the Logos Cube," he mumbled. "As for leaving clues, he may have hoped that people of goodwill—like ourselves—would come to the cottage, find the card in the vase, and carry the cube away so the Autarchs couldn't get it."

"The logic of all this is as full of holes as Swiss cheese," Miss Eells shot back. "And so is your head."

By now Emerson was getting angry. "My dear sister," he said in a strained voice, "I have been right up to now, haven't I? Well, haven't I?"

Miss Eells sighed helplessly. "I suppose . . ." she began uncertainly.

"Well, then," said Emerson triumphantly, "I don't see why you should doubt my intuition and my logic in this case. We have to locate that sundial!"

"Did you see any sundials when we were at the estate last night?" asked Anthony timidly.

Emerson sighed. "No, Anthony, I did not. But I have a good idea of where one might be: in that blasted, infernal garden. You see, the Autarchs have tried to make their world look like an old-fashioned English estate. Years ago I went on a historic houses tour in England, and I recall that many of them had sundials in their gardens. It frightens me to think about it, but we are going to have to go into that garden and find the sundial. It might not be there, but it's the most logical place for one.

"As far as I'm concerned, it'll be about as much fun as going down in the crater of a smoking volcano. But it must be done."

That night, the weather got in the way of Emerson's plans. The day was sunny and chilly, but around sunset the sky clouded over, and the chest failed to appear. Meanwhile, the Autarchs were holding a special meeting. One of their servants, a guard at the estate, had spied on Emerson and the others through one of the windows in the Temple. Later, he had followed them down the path and had watched them get into the chest. At first the guard had been afraid to report to his masters, but he knew that the Grand Autarch could read minds, and he decided that it would go easier with him if he just went in and told what he knew. So the special meeting was called. Candles burned in every wall bracket and sconce, and their yellow wavering light played over the polished mahogany table and the faces of the grotesque black-robed people who ruled this strange, gloomy world. The guard stood near the end of the table where the Grand Autarch sat. Like most of the men who patrolled the estate, this was a young man, and he wore a close-fitting leather jacket studded with iron spikes. His hair was long and yellow, and on one cheek was an ugly scar made by a knife. The Grand Autarch had recruited him personally, on one of his trips to earth. On a visit to the city of Montreal, he had contacted the young man, who had no money and no friends and slept on park benches at night. Now the young guard stood nervously rubbing his hands together as he told his tale. He told of the three strange people who had invaded the Temple of the Winds and how they had taken away a small glittering object—a coin, probably. As the guard talked, the Grand Autarch grew angrier and angrier. His lips curled into a hateful scowl, and he fiddled with the golden chain of office that he wore around his neck. When the guard had finished making his report the Grand Autarch began to speak. He seemed to be struggling to control himself, and there was a tremor in his voice.

"Do you mean to tell me," he began, "that you made no attempt to seize these intruders? No attempt at all?"

The guard stared at the floor. "I couldn't," he said in a frightened voice. "They were carrying some kind of protection with them—amulets, maybe, I don't know. But I couldn't go near them. I could only watch."

The Grand Autarch glowered scornfully. "You could only watch," he repeated in a dangerously calm voice. "You couldn't do a thing. You were helpless. And so those people were able to escape and carry away something that might be of great importance to us."

The guard wiped his sweaty forehead with his hand. "Yes, my lord," he mumbled. "I couldn't help it, as I—"

He never got to finish his sentence. With a loud cry the Grand Autarch rose from his seat and pointed a long bony hand at the guard. The guard screamed in pain, and the air around him turned to gray smoke. When the smoke cleared there stood a hunched old man with drooping wrinkled cheeks and a few wisps of white hair on his head. His eyes were red-rimmed and sunk into deep hollows. His spiked leather uniform hung loosely on his skinny withered body.

"Why did you do this to me?" the guard asked. His voice was cracked and shaky, the voice of a man who might be eighty or ninety years old. "I tried to do my duty, I really did."

The Grand Autarch was still boiling with rage. He clenched his fists and sank back into his seat. "I have punished you because you failed. A true servant of the Autarchs would have found a way to stop three silly, helpless people. And why didn't you come to me immediately after you saw them get away?"

"I was afraid," said the guard, who was weeping helplessly now.

"Why don't you kill him now?" said a nasty-looking old woman who sat at the far end of the table. "I hate to see people suffer."

The Grand Autarch shook his head. "No," he said firmly. "He will water the plants in the garden and rake leaves and do other tasks that are fit for elderly servants. Some day, if I feel that he has suffered enough, I will return him to his former shape. Go, wretch. I am finished with you for now."

The guard turned and shuffled away, still weeping. When the door had closed behind him all the Autarchs began to speak at once.

"What do you suppose they found?"

"We should go after them!"

"We need what they've got! And we need vengeance!"

"Who are they? And how did they find out about this place?"

And so on. Finally the Grand Autarch raised his arms and roared, *"Silence!* I still rule here, and I will deal with the problem in my own way. I will pursue these wretched intruders and make them wish they had never tampered with our world. In fact, I shall go tonight. The meeting is adjourned."

The Autarchs got up and left the Council Room, still muttering to themselves. But the Grand Autarch swept his cloak about him grandly and walked to a place in the paneled wall where carved cherub heads smiled amid clusters of carved grape leaves. Seizing one of the heads between his thumb and his forefinger, the Grand Autarch twisted it, and part of the paneled wall swung inward. Stone steps wound down into darkness, and the Autarch snatched a torch from a bracket just inside the doorway. A muttered word from him made the end of the torch bloom with fire, and down he went, along a corkscrewing passage so narrow that his shoulders almost brushed both walls. At last he came out into a crypt, a large room with heavy stone pillars and ribbed vaulting. Set into the walls were oblong niches, and in many of them were coffins. Brass plates glimmered on the sides of the coffins, showing that a certain Autarch had died on such-and-such a date at such-and-such an age. The grim-faced leader stalked on until he came to an empty wooden coffin that lay in the middle of the floor. Climbing into it, he lay down and crossed his hands over his chest. He muttered a few words in a strange language, and the coffin began to fill with yellow smoke. When the smoke had cleared, the Autarch was gone.

CHAPTER NINE

For the next three days, the sky over Shadow Lake was gray and gloomy. Clouded by day and clouded at night. Emerson and the others felt terribly frustrated, but there wasn't much they could do except wait. Meanwhile, at night Anthony began to hear and see strange things. Once he woke from a sound sleep to hear someone whispering outside his door. Rigid with terror, he sat listening. Who was it? What was the whisperer saying? Anthony could almost make it out, but not quite. He didn't dare go near the door, and after a while the whispering died away. On another night, he heard something tapping at his window. It couldn't be a branch, because there weren't any trees close enough to his window to touch it. Still the tapping went on, and with a sudden cry of fear Anthony rushed to the door and flung it open. There was no one there.

The next morning Anthony looked exhausted—he had hardly slept a wink after the tapping incident. But when Miss Eells asked him if anything was wrong, he merely shrugged and munched his cornflakes. Miss Eells and Emerson knew Anthony pretty well by this time, and they were sure that they would not get anything out of him by pestering him. So they just let the matter drop, and breakfast was eaten in silence.

The rest of the morning was spent cleaning up the cottage. Miss Eells and Anthony did the laundry the old-fashioned way, with tub and washboard and soap flakes. Later they hung the wash out to dry on a clothesline behind the house, while Emerson refilled the kerosene lamps and polished their nickel-plated reflectors. After lunch the three of them played badminton till they were tired, and after a brief nap they went fishing. Emerson steered the boat leisurely around the lake. As he pulled at the oars he wondered if the sky would be clear tonight. In spite of the danger he was itching to go back, because he felt that it was important to follow up the clue scratched on the Brasher doubloon. Besides, Emerson liked danger—it got the blood pumping in his viens, it made him feel alive. But the gray clouds that were rolling in from the west did not make him feel very hopeful—it looked like another night of overcast sky.

When the cottage and its dock came into view, the

three vacationers got a surprise: There, pulled up to the shore, was a rowboat with an outboard motor. And sitting in it was an old white-haired man who calmly puffed a corncob pipe and stared at them with a weary smile, as if to say *At last!* He seemed to be about sixty years old, and his chin was covered with a two days' growth of stubble. He wore a red plaid shirt, gray work pants, muddy combat boots, and a shapeless gray fedora stuck full of fishing flies.

"Evening," said the old man, as Emerson pulled the rowboat nearer.

"Good evening," said Emerson crisply, as he drew alongside the old man's boat. "We're the people who are staying in this cottage. Can we help you?"

The old man sighed. "Well, maybe you can. The truth is, I left my oars at home, and I just found out that I am out of gasoline. So I'll have to ask you to let me stay here tonight or . . . or help me to get home."

Emerson smiled. "As it happens, we can do either one: I have some extra gasoline, and I even have a spare set of oars. You're welcome to share our not-very-special evening meal and sack out in one of the spare rooms till morning or just go on your way. Whatever you want to do, we'll help you with it."

The old man seemed totally overcome by Emerson's offer of hospitality. Tears came to his eyes. "Thank you . . . thank you, sir," he said in a voice thick with emotion. "I was lucky to run into decent folks like yourselves. I will be glad to have dinner with you, and then

I'll put some gas in my tank and go on my way. I live on the other side of the lake. It's not so far."

The old man pulled his boat up onto the shore, and Emerson hooked his to a post on the dock. Later, in the kitchen, they all had a simple meal of baked potatoes, sausage, and tea. As they ate, Emerson seemed to grow very interested in the old man. He looked at his hands a lot, and he also stared at the flies that were stuck in the hat that the old man wore as he gobbled down his food. After dinner Emerson got out a box of cigars and offered the old man one. The man shook his head vigorously and said no—he had decided that cigars were bad for him. Emerson lit one and blew clouds of smoke into the air. Then he looked straight at the old man and said, in an offhand way, "So how are the fish biting on the upper lake? I've heard that the muskellunge are biting up there—not to mention the trout. What do you say?"

At first the old man looked a bit disconcerted, as if Emerson had asked him a very personal question. But he coughed and smiled and folded his hands on the table. "I would say that I've seen better years for fishing," muttered the old man with a scowl. "It's not so good, not so good at all."

But Emerson would not let the subject drop. "Do you have a lot of trouble getting through that narrow channel that connects us with the upper lake? It's choked with reeds—people say you can't go up there with an outboard motor because the reeds foul the propeller."

The old man began to act upset. He got red in the face and glanced out the window at the setting sun. "I . . . . I haven't been up there lately," he mumbled. "The upper lake's fished out, from what I hear."

"Really?" said Emerson smoothly, as he poured himself another cup of coffee. "That's not what I heard."

The old man said nothing. Anthony and Miss Eells looked at each other. What kind of game was Emerson playing? Anthony had seen a lot of reeds at the other end of the lake, but Emerson had never mentioned an upper lake until now. Was he kidding the old guy? Or what?

After a few more sips of coffee, the old man abruptly shoved his chair back and stood up. "Well, I got to go now," he mumbled, and he clumsily held out his hand for Emerson to shake. Emerson smiled blandly and shook the man's hand. "I'll get the gas to fill your engine," he said, as he shoved his chair back. He got up to go to the back room, where the supplies were kept. A few minutes later Emerson came back with a red can that sprouted a long collapsible nozzle. The old man waved his hand at Anthony and Miss Eells as he stumbled out the door after Emerson. The gas tank got filled, and soon the elderly fisherman was on his way, put-putting across the darkening rippled waters of Shadow Lake.

Emerson stood at the end of the dock and watched him go. Behind him stood Anthony and Miss Eells, who both seemed slightly bewildered. "Filthy rotten fake!"

said Emerson aloud, as soon as the man was out of hearing range.

Miss Eells looked at her brother in amazement. "Em, what are you driving at?"

Emerson chuckled grimly. "I'd bet you a million bucks that old coot isn't what he pretends to be. Want to know why?"

Miss Eells looked startled. "Yes, I would. He seemed all right to me."

Emerson folded his arms and looked scornful. "Myra, I've done a lot of fly-fishing, and I have never seen flies that looked like the ones in that man's hat. And did you get a look at his hands? They're not red and rough the way a fisherman's hands ought to be. But that's not all: As you may have guessed by now, there is no upper lake. None at all. I wanted to see how our elderly friend would react if I mentioned this fictional upper lake, and I got the kind of response that I expected——he's pretending. I don't know who or what that old geezer is, but he sure isn't a fisherman!"

Anthony felt cold all over. Some very unpleasant thoughts were forming in his mind. "So . . . who do you think he is, Mr. Eells?" he asked in a quavering voice.

Emerson heaved a deep sigh and dug his hands into his pockets. "I don't know," he said in a low voice. "But it has occurred to me that someone may have spotted us when we were poking around in the Temple of the

Winds. And if that's true, we may be in deep trouble. We may be facing a visitor from that other world—a visitor with vengeance on his mind."

Anthony was feeling very uneasy now. "You . . . you mean those people in the black robes found out that we stole the gold coin, and they want it back?"

Emerson sighed and nodded. "Something like that could be going on, I'm afraid. And I haven't the faintest idea of how we ought to deal with the problem."

Miss Eells looked skeptical. "Em," she said slowly, "aren't you pushing the panic button a little bit early? I mean, that old guy might just be a harmless eccentric, some slightly unbalanced local character who wants all the tourists to think he's a great fly-fisherman and an expert on the local fishing conditions. That would explain the weird flies in his hat and all that nonsense about the upper lake. Well, wouldn't it?"

Emerson said nothing. The clouds in the west parted, and a long ray of reddish light shot out. It hovered over the three figures who stood on the dock, and then it was gone. Darkness deepened on the lake. "I think we are in big trouble," Emerson intoned in a grave voice. "You can explain all you like, but I feel it in my bones. That old man—whoever or whatever he is—will be back. You mark my words, he will! And I'll bet he's after the gold coin. We'll have to hide it somewhere, in a place that's safe. Suggestions, anyone?"

Miss Eells stooped and picked up one of the flat smooth stones that Emerson had plucked from the bed of the lake. She tried to make it skip across the water, but as usual it didn't work for her—the stone sank immediately. "I think we should take the coin out to the middle of the lake and pitch it in," she said at last. "We've got the information we need from it, so it's useless to us now—unless you think you're going to clean up in the rare coin market, Em."

"Well, I sort of had something like that in mind, Myra, if you must know," he said with a sheepish grin on his face. "I mean, even a defaced Brasher doubloon is worth *something*. You might get ten thousand dollars for it, instead of the quarter million that you could expect if it was undamaged. That would be enough money to pay for Anthony's college education."

Miss Eells looked at Emerson in exasperation. "Em, they don't let dead people into college! What I mean is, if you're right about that old guy, then he'll kill us out of pure spite if he can't find the coin. Is it worth it to hide the thing?"

Emerson seemed amused. "So now you've come around to my point of view about the old geezer," he said, chuckling. Then he turned to Anthony, who had not said much lately. "Anthony," Emerson asked, "where would you hide the doubloon?"

Anthony shrugged. "Gee, Mr. Eells, I'd . . . well, there's a loose board in the floor in the parlor. I noticed it because I keep stepping on it. Why don't we put the coin under there?"

Emerson grinned and rubbed his hands together in a

satisfied way. "An excellent suggestion!" he said. "Brilliant! I'll get a clawhammer and draw out the nails in the board. Then we can put the board back when we've hidden the coin."

"I think the two of you are out of your minds," said Miss Eells as she turned to go back to the cottage. "But even lunatics can dry dishes and put them away on shelves. Come on. We've got some cleaning up to do."

After the dishes were done, Emerson and Anthony got the loose floorboard up in the study, and they laid the coin down on the dirt under the parlor floor. Then Emerson replaced the board and banged the nails back into place. Later the three vacationers tried to spend a normal evening in the parlor. Miss Eells and Anthony played gin rummy, and Emerson played Gilbert and Sullivan tunes on the upright piano. It was a warm night, and all the downstairs windows were open. A stiff breeze was blowing, and every time a branch swished against the side of the house or an acorn rolled down the roof, Miss Eells would turn and stare wildly toward the door. Once when the waves on the lake bumped their rowboat against the dock, Miss Eells made a little nervous cry and ran to the glass-paned door. She flung it open and stepped out onto the porch. Nobody there.

"Good heavens, Myra!" exclaimed Emerson, turning around on the piano stool. "You're giving everyone the heebie-jeebies the way you're acting! Do you really think that old man—or whoever he is—will come barging in here while we're still up? He won't return until he thinks we're asleep."

"And do you think any of us is going to sleep a wink tonight?" asked Miss Eells, as she walked back into the parlor. "I'm planning on having a nervous breakdown. How about you?"

Emerson got up and brushed lint off the sleeves of his shirt. "Well, Myra," he said calmly, "you can do what you like. I am going to sit all night on the front porch with an ax handle in my hands. I think our friend will show up, and I want to be there to greet him."

Miss Eells was really beginning to worry about her brother's sanity now. "Emerson!" she exclaimed. "If there's someone from that otherworld coming to get the coin, do you really think you can defend yourself with an ax handle? Use your brain, for heaven's sake."

"I am using my brain," snapped Emerson. "And I have a little theory about how much power that old coot might have. But see here, it's almost eleven o'clock. Why don't the two of you go to bed, and I'll stand guard. You're not going to help by pacing back and forth and chewing your lips."

Miss Eells stared helplessly at Emerson for a few seconds. Then she went around the room and turned off all the oil lamps except one. Meanwhile Anthony lit a couple of candles so the two of them could find their way up to bed. Emerson went around to the back of the house and opened the rattly door of the toolshed. With flashlight in hand, he poked around till he found a stout smooth ax handle. Then he made his way back around to the front of the house again. After putting out the last oil lamp, he went out to the front porch, turned off his flashlight, and sat down to wait.

Minutes dragged past. A quarter of an hour, then a half hour went by. The parlor windows were open, so Emerson could hear the ticking of the shelf clock and its loud, hoarse croaking when it struck the half hours and hours. Outside it was totally dark. Emerson heard the crickets in the tall grass, and now and then he saw a streak of moonlight on the rippled waters of the lake. This light broke through when the clouds parted briefly. But then they would rush in to close up the gap, and the darkness would continue. Humming softly, Emerson gripped the ax handle in his right hand and tapped it calmly on his knee. Midnight passed, and so did twelve-thirty in the morning. By now Emerson's eyes had gotten used to the darkness, and he could make out the narrow, oblong shape of the dock and their boat, bumping gently against the pilings. Suddenly Emerson heard the dip and splash of oars. A rowboat was gliding in past the dock to the shore, and Emerson could see a shadowy figure inside it. The bow of the rowboat ground into the soft sand, and the figure leapt out to pull it up farther. Even in the dark Emerson could tell that the person coming toward him was not the old fisherman. It was someone tall and lean, someone who wore a long cape or robe. Gripping the ax handle tightly, Emerson sat up in his chair. He felt the blood singing in his ears.

"Who is it?" he called out.

No answer. The figure strode swiftly forward, and soon it was on the path that led to the porch. Crunch, crunch went the gravel as the menacing shape stepped forward. At the foot of the cracked wooden steps it halted.

"I am the Grand Autarch," the deep voice intoned. "And I have come to take back the object that you stole from my domain. Give it to me."

The Grand Autarch! Emerson realized that he must be speaking to the tall, hunched figure with the golden chain around his neck, the one who had been sitting at the head of the table in the Council Chamber of the mansion. Because he had seen the Autarch only through the peephole in the wall, Emerson had not gotten a really good look at this man. Probably he would get a better look in a minute.

"The Grand Autarch!" said Emerson, and then he laughed mockingly. "How about that! Is that anything like a Grand Dragon? Are you with the Ku Klux Klan, or what?"

The Grand Autarch seemed disconcerted by this mockery, but he wrapped his cloak about him and spoke again in a menacing tone. "Little man, you do not understand your peril. I could shrivel you to a cinder with a single gesture of my hand. But I will be merciful if you give that golden trinket to me. *Now!*"

"I don't think I've ever been shriveled to a cinder," said Emerson carelessly. "It'd be a new experience. But look here, you're trespassing on private property, and you're interfering with the sleep of my household. I don't have anything for you, so I would suggest that you just clear out. Besides, you're beginning to bore me. Go on— scram!"

Silence. The Autarch said nothing. For a full minute the two of them faced each other in silence. Then Emerson saw the cape swirl, and he thought he caught the glimmer of a knife blade. *"Aaaaaah!"* roared the Autarch, and he rushed up the steps with a wicked-looking dagger held on high. Emerson stepped nimbly to one side and whacked the man on the shoulder with the ax handle. The Autarch groaned with pain and fell to his knees. Then he struggled back to his feet, and Emerson hit him on the other shoulder. Frightened and angry, the Autarch tried once more to stab Emerson with the dagger. But Emerson brought the ax handle down on his wrist, and the dagger clattered to the boards of the porch.

"This . . . is kind of getting . . . to be fun," panted Emerson, as he backed up against the wall of the house and waited for the Autarch's next move. "You were better off as an old fisherman, and I would suggest that you turn back into one and scoot. Or haven't you had enough?"

The Autarch rubbed his sore shoulder and stumbled back down the steps to the path. "I'll make you wish that you had never been born, little man," he snarled. "Being skinned alive would be a picnic compared to what I'm going to do to you. Just wait."

"I can wait," said Emerson placidly. "Your threats mean nothing to me. But if you're not out of here in two minutes, I'm going to come down there and beat knobs on your head. Understand?"

The Autarch paused a moment more. Then, turning abruptly, he strode off the path and made his way through the long grass to the place where his boat was pulled up onto the sand. After a little struggling he shoved the boat out onto the lake and climbed in. Once more Emerson heard the sound of oars splashing as the rowboat disappeared into the blackness.

"Oh, good Lord!" breathed Emerson, as he mopped his face with his handkerchief. "Mercy upon us all! *It worked!*"

Two figures popped up from the place where they had been crouching, below the parlor windows. Anthony and Miss Eells had not really gone to bed. In stocking feet, they had tiptoed down the back staircase and crept along the hall till they reached the parlor windows. From there they had listened to the strange battle between Emerson and the menacing creature from another world.

Miss Eells stumbled out onto the porch, with Anthony close behind her. "What worked?" Miss Eells asked in a bewildered tone.

Emerson heaved a deep sigh. After the fight he seemed

weary, but he tried to act as if he was in control of the situation. "I guessed that the Autarch would be practically powerless in our world. Otherwise, why would he bother to make himself look like an old fisherman? Anyone who can fry someone's brains with a gesture doesn't need to use trickery to get what he wants. Or knives, for that matter. So I decided that I could push him around."

"But how come you were so sure?" asked Anthony, who was amazed at Emerson's calmness in the face of danger.

Anthony raised the beam of his flashlight, and he saw that Emerson's face looked drawn and haggard. Beads of sweat stood out on his forehead. Once again Anthony asked his question. "How did you know? Weren't you afraid?"

"I . . . I wasn't sure at all," said Emerson faintly, "Not . . . not until I tried." And with that he collapsed in a heap on the splintery boards.

CHAPTER TEN

A few minutes later Emerson awoke. Anthony had placed a folded jacket under his head for a pillow, and Miss Eells was waving a bottle of smelling salts under his nose. Emerson coughed and sputtered and glanced blearily around. He was not the fainting type—or so he thought—so his present situation really embarrassed him.

"I . . . I seem to have collapsed," said Emerson vaguely. He struggled to his feet. "So our nasty enemy is gone," he muttered, as he brushed lint off his sleeves. "Let us hope that . . ."

Suddenly there was a sound of glass breaking. In a flash Emerson guessed. So did Anthony and Miss Eells.

"Good God!" exclaimed Emerson, clapping his hand to his mouth. "You don't suppose . . ."

Without another word Emerson, Miss Eells, and Anthony dashed up the front stairs and down the narrow hall. They stopped in front of the door of the room where the chest sometimes appeared. From a small table in the hall Emerson snatched a candle, and after a little scrabbling in a drawer he found some matches and lit it. Into the room he stepped, followed by the other two. Emerson walked straight toward the window and raised his candle high. What everyone expected turned out to be true—the purple pane was shattered. Pieces of violet colored glass lay on the floor of the room. And there was the small rock that had done the damage. The magic chest would never return to this room, no matter how brightly Arcturus shone. This pathway to another world was blocked forever.

Emerson was trembling with rage. He stood there silently staring at the broken windowpane. The candle shook in his clenched fist, and his shoulders hunched up as his whole body grew tense. Then Emerson let all his anger out in one long, shuddering sigh. He stooped and picked up one of the broken glass fragments.

"Well, I guess that's about it," he said. Letting the glass shard fall back to the floor, Emerson turned back to his friends. "I suppose we could glue the pieces together," he said glumly. "But I have always heard that the magic flows out of an enchanted object once it has been broken. We may as well pack up and head for Hoosac. I was getting tired of this vacation anyway."

Miss Eells stepped forward and touched her brother sympathetically on the arm. "Maybe it's all for the best, Em," she said softly. "You've cheated the odds twice by going to that place. Anthony has cheated them three times. But eventually the law of averages would have caught up to us. We would probably all have been killed before we found that Whatchamajigger Cube."

"Logos Cube," said Emerson, who hated to hear people use the wrong names to identify things.

"I think Miss Eells is right," Anthony put in. "And anyway, I don't really think those creeps can take over our world. They'll have to stay where they are."

Emerson glanced at Anthony, and he looked as if he was about to say something, but then he changed his mind and led the way out of the room. In silence the three of them clumped down the stairs and then walked around, fastening the first floor windows and bolting the doors. When this was done, each took a candle and climbed the steps to bed. As he wearily took off his clothes, Anthony thought that he would be glad to be back home in good old Hoosac. But this was only partly true. Anthony didn't like the danger they had been put into, but there was still a large question floating around in his mind: Had they seen the last of the evil mansion and its sinister inhabitants? If they had found the Logos Cube and smashed it, then they would be sure they were safe. As it was now, they would never know . . . until it was too late.

The next day the three vacationers packed up their things and straightened up the old cottage for the final time. They locked the doors and threw their luggage into Emerson's boat, and soon they were putting across the quiet waters of the lake. It was late August, but a chill was in the air, and leaves had already started to turn. Autumn was coming to this lonely northern outpost. Emerson steered toward the little settlement on the north side of the lake. It wasn't much—just a few houses, a trading post, a church, and the local headquarters of the Royal Canadian Mounted Police. When they got there Emerson went straight to the Mounties' headquarters and explained that he and his friends needed to get home as quickly as they could. The officer on duty told him that a pontoon plane would be arriving around one in the afternoon, and for a fee the pilot would take them to the town of Withers, where they could catch a train to Montreal. From there they could fly to Minneapolis, which was only a hundred miles from Hoosac. So Emerson sold his rowboat and the outboard motor, and they settled down at the trading post to wait for the plane.

A few days later the three of them were back home, going about the normal routine of their lives. Anthony wandered about the town during the day and shelved books at the library at night. When his parents asked how his trip had been, he shrugged carelessly and said that it had been "all right." That was the most that they could get out of him. Mrs. Monday was disappointed that he had not brought back any postcards or souvenirs—but then Anthony had never cared much for things like that.

August turned to September, and the usual breathless muggy heat of late summer stayed on and on. After Labor Day Anthony went back to school. But the dark mansion and its evil inhabitants stayed in his mind. What were they doing in their moonlit world? What sort of nastiness were they plotting? Emerson was pretty sure that the Grand Autarch had smashed the purple windowpane, and he was also convinced that the chest was not the only pathway between our world and the other one. If it had been, the Autarch would hardly have done something that would leave him stranded in northern Canada. There had to be another way, one that only the Autarchs knew of. But Emerson had searched the island before they left, and he had found nothing but trees and rocks and weeds. Maybe now the Autarchs would stay in their little kingdom and not bother the inhabitants of Earth. Maybe—but Anthony had his doubts.

A week went by. The heat wave broke and autumn winds began to blow in the valley of the Upper Mississippi. The leaves on the tall wooded bluffs turned and began to fall. One sleepy Saturday afternoon Anthony was sitting in a window seat in the Hoosac Public Library. He had a feather duster in his hand, but he had gotten tired of dusting, so he just sat and watched the wind strip the yellow leaves from the elm trees across the street. The library was nearly empty. Old Mr. Beemis was in the East Reading Room playing chess with one of his friends, and a grim old woman in a black dress was up at the front desk arguing with Miss Eells about some adventure novels that she felt were not fit for young people to read. Because they were in a library, the argument had to be carried on in whispers, and this amused Anthony. From where he was sitting he could see the two of them wagging their jaws at each other, though he couldn't make out what they were saying. Finally the woman turned and stalked away. Anthony heard the inner doors of the library hiss shut behind her. With the duster still in his hand, he ambled toward the main desk. Miss Eells was shaking her head and laughing quietly. When she saw Anthony approaching she smiled, but then another laughing fit came over her. When it was over she sighed and wiped her face with a lace-trimmed handkerchief.

"Oh, my Lord!" she said, shaking her head. "That woman belongs in an institution! If we did what she wanted, there'd be a huge bonfire of books out behind the library. Fortunately everybody on the Library Board thinks she's a nut, so I suppose she's harmless. But I can't help arguing with her, all the same."

Anthony frowned. He had a favor to ask. "Miss Eells?"

"Yes, Anthony? What is it?"

"Do . . . well, do you think maybe we could get out

of here early today? It's nice out, and I think it would be fun to take a drive down the river."

Miss Eells laughed again. This was one of those days when everything seemed to strike her as funny. Then she pulled herself together and tried to act businesslike. "Anthony," she said quietly, "if I closed up shop and got out of this place every time I felt like it, I'd be out of a job pretty soon. I'm afraid I'm stuck here till four, when Miss Pratt comes in to relieve me. But if you'd like a late afternoon jaunt down the river, I'd be delighted. Why don't you call up your folks and tell them that you'll be having dinner with me? We can go south a little way and then angle off into the hinterlands and maybe take some roads we've never been on before. Then we'll come back and stuff ourselves at Reifschneider's, that wonderful German restaurant where you, Emerson, and I ate once. Sauerbraten and red cabbage and the works! Sound good?"

Anthony nodded enthusiastically. "Sounds great!" He glanced over his shoulder at the big electric clock that hung over the main doorway of the library. It said five after two. "I'll go find something to do," he said cheerfully. "The Winterborn Room does need dusting, and somebody spilled a Coke on the floor in the smoking room, so there's sticky stuff next to one of the armchairs. See you."

Anthony did a lot of cleaning up tasks, and Miss Eells read one of the rip-roaring adventure novels that the old lady had condemned. Time passed, and at last four o'clock arrived. Mr. Beemis left, and Anthony and Miss Eells followed as soon as Miss Pratt walked in. Soon they were driving down a two-lane road that ran on the Wisconsin side of the Mississippi river. Above them loomed tall limestone bluffs where trees waved in the wind. Now and then a shower of red and yellow leaves would come drifting down onto the car, which was still wet from the morning's rain. They drove on, singing football songs, like "Buckle Down Winsocki," "On Wisconsin!" and "The Notre Dame Victory March." After half an hour they came to a side road that angled off through a cleft in the bluffs. A wooden sign said:

NEW STOCKHOLM 13 mi.

DANZIG 6 mi.

ARETHA 28 mi.

Miss Eells slowed down and turned left onto the narrow side road. "I've never been to any of these towns," she said in answer to Anthony's questioning look. "And considering how long I've lived in these parts, it's high time that I investigated one or two of them. Okay by you?"

Anthony said yes, it was fine. He liked to explore, and he knew that Miss Eells didn't mind getting lost. So he just settled back and enjoyed the scenery. First they passed through rugged country where steep hills rose on either side of them. Here and there they would see a collapsing barn, or a deserted farmhouse with boarded windows, or a lonely gas station with cars rusting to pieces in a field nearby. They passed through Danzig, which had a gas station, a general store, a Grange Hall, and a few houses huddled together. That was it— not even a post office. On they drove, as the sun sank lower in the west. Finally they came to New Stockholm, which was a bit bigger than Danzig—about 500 people, Miss Eells guessed. It was clear that the town had once seen better days: The Masonic Temple was quite a production, with stone lions in front, a red granite staircase, and a greenish copper cornice on the roof. And on the side streets were some old mansions that had probably belonged to rich people years ago. Anthony loved old houses and always tried to imagine who had lived in them and what their lives had been like.

Suddenly Anthony gasped.

Miss Eells pulled over to the side of the road, stopped the car, and turned off the motor. She turned to Anthony, who looked pale and frightened. "Good heavens, Anthony!" said Miss Eells in a worried voice. "Whatever is the matter?"

Anthony sat rigidly still, staring at the windshield. "Turn around and go back a little ways and you'll find out what's the matter," he muttered. "Across the way and to the right down a side street. That's where it is."

Miss Eells wanted to ask, "Where *what* is?" but she didn't. Instead she revved up the car and looked up and down the road. Nobody was coming, so she did a U-turn and cruised slowly back down the main street of the town.

"This street," said Anthony faintly. "Off to your right."

Miss Eells swerved onto a rutty side street and then suddenly, like Anthony, she gasped. "Oh, my good Lord in heaven!" she said. "I see what you mean. This is incredible!"

Miss Eells stopped the car next to a fire hydrant, and the two of them got out. Then they just stared for a long while. They were looking at a three-story black stone mansion with narrow windows and a slate roof. The tall chimneys were capped by iron chimney covers that looked like Chinese pagoda roofs. They could see the south side of the building, which was thick with tangled vines, and level with the ground was a false stone doorway with a Greek cornice. Next to it stood a headless statue of a woman in a toga. Her marble arm pointed up. And a little way off to the left were the tangled, weedy remains of a garden.

"It's . . . it's . . ." quavered Miss Eells, but she couldn't finish the sentence. She didn't have to—Anthony knew, as she did, that they were staring at a house that was like the mansion they had seen in that misty moonlit otherworld.

After opening and closing his mouth a few times, Anthony finally found that he could speak. "I wonder what it means," he said in a choked voice.

"I don't know," replied Miss Eells quietly. "This is all very, very strange. We'll have to tell Emerson about it. Before we go, though, I'd like a slightly closer look."

Anthony was terrified. He grabbed Miss Eells's arm. "You're not going *in* there, are you?" he gasped. "Please don't! Please, please don't!"

"Of course I'm not going in!" said Miss Eells. "I may be weird and impractical, but I'd like to live a few more years. I just want to walk to the main gate and see if I can see any signs of life. Are you with me?"

Anthony nodded, and he followed Miss Eells along the spike-topped iron fence that surrounded the mansion's grounds. The empty windows stared out silently at them, and once they were startled by a crow that suddenly took off from one of the chimneys. It flew past, cawing loudly. Soon Anthony and Miss Eells came to a padlocked gate and two tall black stone gateposts with lanterns on top. The frosted panes of the lanterns were broken; there was a wooden sign wired to the gate. It said:

FOR SALE

Hjalmarson Realtors

Phone: 6854

Anthony noticed two more weathered FOR SALE signs. They were lying in the tall grass just inside the gateway, and they had the names of other real estate companies on them. Apparently it had been hard to sell this depressing old place.

Miss Eells peered through the bars at the tall porch of the mansion. It was narrow, just a flattopped canopy over the front door, held up by square-edged wooden posts. "I've never seen the main entrance of that other mansion," she said. "Have you, Anthony?"

Anthony shook his head. "No, I haven't," he said. Then he added in an odd voice, "I'll bet they're both the same."

"No bet," said Miss Eells grimly. She folded her arms and went on gazing at this strange abandoned building. After another long look she turned away. "Come on, Anthony," she said softly, as she touched him on the arm. "We'd better be getting back home. It's after five, and we'll be lucky to make it to Reifschneider's before the dinnertime crowd."

CHAPTER ELEVEN

That evening after dinner Miss Eells phoned her brother Emerson and told him about the discovery that she and Anthony had made. Needless to say, Emerson was surprised. He was also a little bit frightened.

"Look, Myra," he said, talking rapidly as he always did when he was excited, "find out whatever you can about the former owner of that mansion. I'll bet that it was the Grand Autarch himself, though I doubt that was the name he used when he lived in New Stockholm. The really interesting thing about your discovery is that it gives us hope."

Miss Eells was mystified. "*Hope?* What kind of hope?"

"If the mansion in the Autarchs' world is a copy of the one you saw," said Emerson, "then maybe inside it is something we could use the way we used the magic chest. Do you understand what I'm saying?"

"Brother dear," Miss Eells said, "your logic escapes me. Why should there be anything magical inside that old run-down heap of a house? I'd expect cobwebs and mice, perhaps, but not magic chests that travel between dimensions."

"I'm not being logical, I'm playing a hunch," said Emerson. "And anyway, it's the only hope we have of getting back to the Autarchs' world."

Miss Eells shuddered. "Why ever would we want to do that? I thought that whole episode was over and done with. Are you still thinking about the Logic Cube, or whatever it's called?"

"Yes, Myra, I am," said Emerson. "Do you really think those black-robed creeps are going to sit back and forget about the cube? It's changing their world without their permission. Also, they have a plan for taking over *our* world—remember, I heard it with my own ears—and they can't do it without the cube. Do you think I can sleep nights while there's a chance they might find the cursed thing and work unimaginable magic with it?"

Miss Eells heaved a despairing sigh. She knew Emerson, and when he was convinced that he was right, you couldn't argue with him. Also, Miss Eells had to admit that what he was saying made a weird sort of sense. Maybe the world was in danger, and maybe they had better find a way to get the cube before the Autarchs found it. "Very well, Em," she said at last. "I'll go back up to New Stockholm and try to find out about the former owner of that ugly old dump. Maybe I can pretend to be someone who wants to buy the place."

"Sounds like a good idea," said Emerson. "You find out what you can, and call me immediately if you discover something. I have a few wills to draw up, but there's nothing that can't be shoved aside for a few days if I absolutely have to come down there. Good luck." And with that he hung up.

"Good luck indeed!" muttered Miss Eells to herself, as she put the receiver back in its cradle. "I wonder what I have gotten myself into?" Then she decided to call up Anthony and tell him about Emerson's latest idea.

The very next Saturday afternoon, Miss Eells and Anthony found themselves standing in the front hall of the mansion in New Stockholm, Wisconsin. The real estate agent was a short cheerful man who wore a checkered sport coat and a handpainted tie that looked like a sunset in the tropics. He had a thin mustache, was nearly bald, and he smelled of cheap cigars. Miss Eells didn't like him, but she smiled politely and tried to seem interested as the man went on about the old house and its wonderful qualities. Who had lived here before? A guy by the name of Ambrose. Marius F. Ambrose, that was his name. He had disappeared mysteriously in the mid-1930's, and the house had become the property of a cousin named Harlow Fredberg, who very much wanted to sell it to someone who would take good care of it. And how much was he asking? Only $20,000.

A steal it was, for a grand place like this, an absolute steal! Genuine hardwood floors, wainscots covered with real leather, and lots of very fine wood carving that showed Old World craftsmanship. And the fireplaces, well, they were . . .

"Could we see the house?" Miss Eells cut in. She didn't mean to be rude, but she knew that they'd be here all day if she didn't get pushy.

The agent gave her a look—he was enjoying the sound of his own voice, and he hated to be interrupted. But he shrugged and led his two customers into the house. They trekked through room after room where furniture lay shrouded in gray dustcovers. Living room, back parlor, dining room, kitchen, pantry. It was a house meant for rich people who paid an army of servants to keep the place tidy and serve meals. *Those days are gone forever, thank God!* said Miss Eells to herself. She had never been able to afford servants, but it didn't matter anyway. She hated being waited on by anyone. They climbed the main staircase to the landing above. Suddenly Miss Eells stopped. As soon as Anthony saw the dusky oil painting that hung in a gilt frame on the wall, he knew why they were pausing.

The painting showed a tall, gloomy-looking man in a frock coat, wing collar, and black string tie. His forehead was high, and his red-rimmed eyes burned below arched black eyebrows. His nose was long and ridged, and a pair of pince-nez glasses hung by a black ribbon from his lapel. He was standing behind a small table—

a writing desk it was, actually, with a slanted top and a low railing on three sides. The man's right hand was stuck into the pocket of his jacket; his left hand pointed at some playing cards that lay before him on the table: the three, seven, nine, and ace of spades. All the cards were right side up, facing the man who was pointing at them—except for the ace, which was upside down. Behind the man, the painter had sketched in part of a bookcase lost in shadows, and over his left shoulder a small pointed window could be seen. It was topped by three round panes, that reminded Anthony of the clubs on playing cards:

For a long time Miss Eells studied the painting. She had only seen the Grand Autarch once, when he was standing on the dark pathway in front of the cottage. But Anthony had gotten a better look at the evil man, so she turned to him and gave him a questioning look. Anthony knew what she meant, and he nodded solemnly. That was all Miss Eells needed, and she turned abruptly to the agent.

"Is this a picture of Mr. Ambrose, the former owner of the house?" she asked.

"Yes!" said the agent eagerly. "And a very good likeness, if I do say so myself. It's quite an unusual item, and the experts say that it could command a large price in an auction." The agent was lying—he had always been told that the painting was worthless, but if this silly old woman was willing to pay a lot for it . . .

Miss Eells's voice cut in on the agent's greedy thoughts. "I guess we've seen enough of the picture," she snapped. "Would you show us the rest of the house?"

The agent flinched, but he forced himself to smile. He didn't like Miss Eells, but if she was crazy enough to take the mansion off his company's hands, he might get a handsome commission. "Very well, madam," he said stiffly. "If you will just follow me . . ."

After the tour of the house was over, Miss Eells forced herself to smile and shake the agent's hand. "Thank you so much for showing us this *fascinating* house," she said with fake sweetness. "I'm not sure it's within my price range, but if I think I can afford it, I'll give you a call." And with that, she and Anthony hurried out the door.

Anthony was glad to get out of the place, which was beginning to give him the creeps. Maybe it was the resemblance to the other mansion, or maybe there was some evil presence in the house. Whatever the reason was, he kept expecting to see the evil Autarch every time he turned a corner. So as they drove away, he heaved a sigh of relief.

"Have you had enough of Grisly Grange?" asked Miss Eells with a chuckle. "Wouldn't you love to live there, Anthony?"

Anthony winced. "I'd like to buy some dynamite and

blow the place up," he said vehemently. Then he paused and looked fearfully at Miss Eells. "Emerson doesn't really think that . . . that . . ." he began falteringly.

"He does indeed," said Miss Eells glumly. "He believes that somewhere inside that house is a way back to the misty moonlit world where the Autarchs live. Well, I didn't see anything like a magic chest, did you? No, I didn't think so. There was, however, that weird painting, which may interest Emerson. I suppose I'd better tell him about it."

That evening when Miss Eells phoned her brother, she gave him an account of her visit to the mansion, and she described the painting in great detail. Throughout most of Miss Eells's tale, Emerson had sat silent. Now and then he made little grunts and uh-huh noises, but that was all. But when he heard about the painting he got so excited that Miss Eells thought he would jump through the telephone wires and land in the room next to her.

"Myra!" he crowed. "That painting is just what we want! Nasty old Mr. Ambrose was leaving a clue for those who could read it! How about that!"

Miss Eells covered her face with her hand—she had been afraid of getting some reaction like this. "Emerson," she said patiently, "when you're through turning somersaults will you kindly explain to me what you're talking about? *What* is the painting a clue to?"

"Oh, Myra," exclaimed Emerson impatiently. "Those

cards on the table are probably there for a reason. Three, seven, and nine are magic numbers, and the suit of spades is very important in cartomancy."

"In *what*?" Miss Eells had never heard this word before.

Emerson sighed despairingly. "Cartomancy is the art of using playing cards for magic purposes—like telling fortunes. Ancient wizards used playing cards to cause storms and defeat armies. Enchanted cards arranged in a certain way could open a pathway to the world of the Autarchs. Do you get it?"

Miss Eells was twisting the telephone cord in her hands. "No, frankly I *don't* see!" she said. "Couldn't those cards have been put into the painting as . . . well, just as a decoration? I think you're jumping to conclusions."

Miss Eells and Emerson argued on, and because they both were stubborn they merely succeeded in putting themselves in a foul-tempered state. Finally Emerson said that he was going to get to the bottom of the painting's mystery. He would call up the real estate agent and find out if the table shown in the painting was still in the house. After that . . . well, he wasn't exactly sure what he was going to do, but he said he'd let Miss Eells and Anthony know before he took any steps.

"Before you decide to get yourself killed, you mean!" snapped Miss Eells.

Emerson laughed. "Oh, come on, Myra! First you tell me that my theory about the painting is a lot of garbage, and then you claim that I'm heading into danger. Well, if I'm wrong about the painting, there's no danger, is there?"

Miss Eells had had enough of this conversation, so she hung up. With a worried look on her face she went to her front door and opened it. A cold autumn rain was falling, and the drizzly gloom of the evening suited Miss Eells's mood exactly—she cared about Emerson a lot, and she was always worrying that some harebrained scheme of his would get him into trouble. She didn't want to believe in his ideas about the painting of Mr. Ambrose, but when she thought calmly she had to admit that there was some logic in what he said.

"I hope he's wrong!" said Miss Eells aloud, as she closed the door. "For his sake and Anthony's and mine, I really hope he is!"

September ended with foul weather, as howling gales whipped the trees and roofs of Hoosac. Each day, as he struggled toward the library through wind and blowing leaves, Anthony wondered if Emerson had found out anything about the house in New Stockholm and the mysterious painting of Mr. Ambrose. But whenever he asked Miss Eells, she shrugged and said, "No, there's nothing new." Anthony began to think that Emerson's wonderful theory was wrong, and like Miss Eells, he secretly hoped that Emerson *was* mistaken. But just as Anthony was beginning to feel a bit more relaxed and secure, something happened. He had spent a long evening watching television with his family, and when he dragged himself off to bed he figured that he would sleep like a baby. But around one in the morning he dreamed that someone was knocking on his bedroom door. Instantly he awoke and sat up in bed. The room was silent, and he realized that he had been the victim of a bad dream. But just as he was snuggling down under the warm blanket again, Anthony began to hear whispering. This was not a dream—it was real. Throwing back the covers Anthony sat up. Beads of cold sweat stood out on his forehead, and he could hear his heart thumping. Without knowing why he did this Anthony climbed out of bed and shuffled toward the door. He didn't want to open it, because he was afraid of what he might see on the other side. So he pressed his ear to the varnished wood, and at last the words became clear. And what he heard chilled him to the bone.

CHAPTER TWELVE

The excited soft voice told Anthony that he was in very great danger. If he went back to the world of the moonlit mansion, he would suffer horribly. He wouldn't just die—no, nothing quite as merciful as that. But his spirit would be smothered inside a statue of stone forever and ever. He would beg to die, but the Autarchs would not let it happen. Instead, he would suffer a long drawn-out death, an agonizing living death that would last for hundreds and hundreds of years. It would be worse than the most horrible torture that anyone could possibly imagine.

As Anthony listened to these ominous words, he felt very, very frightened. He wanted to run away, but he couldn't—his feet stayed rooted to the floor, his ears took in every horrid syllable. When the voice finally died away Anthony slumped into a heap on the cold floorboards, and that was where he awoke in the morning, blinking at the bright sunlight that streamed through his bedroom windows. Anthony shook his head groggily and struggled to his feet. He moved slowly toward his bed and sat down. What was it that he had heard? Was it the ghost of one of those three poor vacationers who had been turned to stone statues in the garden next to the Autarchs' mansion? There were a lot of questions spinning around in Anthony's weary brain, but he told himself that he should keep quiet about the whole experience. He would never tell his brother Keith or his parents, because they wouldn't believe him. Miss Eells and Emerson would take him seriously, but if they heard what the whisperer had said, they might make him stay home the next time they went on some wild adventure. The things that had happened to him up at the lonely Canadian cottage made him feel a little differently about things. He was the one who had discovered the chest and the password that activated it. He had gone to that strange otherworld alone, had spied on the Autarchs, and had learned something of their frightening plans. He had even gone back later with Emerson to find out more. Now that Anthony looked back on these experiences, they made him feel courageous and important. Most of the time he was the sort of kid who didn't feel that he was worth much. That was why he was proud of the frightening experiences that he had had. And if

Emerson went back to the magic kingdom of the Autarchs, Anthony wanted to be there at his side.

Weeks passed. Miss Eells fed little tidbits of information to Anthony now and then: The table that appeared in the painting was not in the house any more—it had turned out to be a valuable antique, so it had been sold. But the name of the buyer had been kept secret. There was no way of tracing the table. To Anthony it was as if a door had been slammed in their faces. He was sure Emerson felt the same. He also knew from the way Miss Eells was acting that she was relieved. Whenever he saw her at the library she was extremely cheerful. She even hummed little tunes as she went about her business. Miss Eells's behavior just made Anthony more and more grumpy and frustrated—why did she have to be so happy, just because their adventure was probably over?

October slid by, and Halloween approached. One evening when Anthony was shoving a heavy cart of books down an aisle of the library, Miss Eells surprised him by asking if he wanted to be a waiter at a party that Mrs. Oxenstern was giving. Mrs. Oxenstern was the head of the Hoosac Library Board and she was quite bossy. She and Miss Eells never liked each other very much. In fact, Mrs. Oxenstern would have fired Miss Eells many years ago if she had been able to, but Miss Eells had an ironclad contract that guaranteed her job for life. Lately the two of them had tried to get along

better, and as a gesture of goodwill Miss Eells had volunteered to show up at Mrs. Oxenstern's annual Halloween party. Furthermore, she had offered to bring
members of the library staff in to help—that was why
she was talking to Anthony, who was not exactly thrilled
by the idea of working for Mrs. Oxenstern.

"It's not as if you'll be actually *working* for Mrs. O.,"
said Miss Eells with an encouraging smile. "You'll be
working for *all* of us, the whole library staff, and you'll
be helping to build better relations between the staff
and the Library Board. Then they'll give us more money
and we'll be able to buy more books and maybe put a
new roof on this old wreck of a building. Doesn't that
sound like a good idea to you?"

Anthony grunted. He knew that he would give in
and work at the party, but not for any of the reasons
that Miss Eells had given him—he would do it because
of his loyalty to her. And so on the evening of October
31 Anthony found himself in a waiter's uniform, serv-
ing glasses of pink punch at Mrs. Oxenstern's party.
Mrs. Oxenstern lived in a twenty-three-room mansion
in the nicest part of town, and her living room was
enormous—at one end of it was the table with the
punchbowl, and near it was another table loaded with
goodies of all sorts: canapés, plates of sliced ham and
chicken and smoked tongue, deviled eggs, cheese and
crackers, goose liver paté, and stacks of cucumber sand-
wiches.

Anthony glanced toward the other end of the room. Miss Eells was wearing her best dress, and she was trying very hard to be sociable. She nodded and smiled at practically everything that was said to her, though it was clear to Anthony that she hated every minute of the evening and couldn't wait for it to be over. *That goes for me too*, thought Anthony, as he filled another cup of punch.

Later in the evening another waiter took over Anthony's job for a while, so he could go out on the veranda and get some fresh air. But as he walked toward the French doors Anthony stopped suddenly. He had seen something that made his face flush and set his heart to beating wildly. Immediately he dashed across the room to find Miss Eells. She was standing with her back to him, listening patiently to a long-winded story that was being told by another guest. Anthony reached out and touched Miss Eells on the shoulder, and she jumped. The coffee cup in her hand rocked dangerously back and forth in its saucer, but luckily it didn't fall.

"Anthony!" exclaimed Miss Eells, as she turned around. "What on earth . . ."

Miss Eells's voice died away when she saw the look on Anthony's face. It was pretty clear that he had something important to tell her that probably needed to be told in private.

"Yes, Anthony?" said Miss Eells in her most polite voice. "What can I do for you?"

"I . . . I have something to show you," said Anthony, who was trying hard to fight down the excitement that was welling up inside him.

"Well, it'll have to wait a few minutes," said Miss Eells sweetly. "I'm listening to a *fascinating* story, and I don't want to miss any of it."

Anthony grimaced. He hated when Miss Eells tried to play Perfect Hostess—she always overdid it, and he could hardly wait for her to behave like her normal everyday self. "Okay, I'll talk to you later," said Anthony curtly, and he turned away. He went back to the punch table and thanked the other boy for giving him a break. A few minutes later, Miss Eells walked up to Anthony with an apologetic smile on her face.

"I'm sorry I had to act like such a drip," she said as Anthony filled her cup. "They expect you to be so polite at these gatherings, and it's driving me *bats!* So what's so important?"

Anthony swallowed hard. "It's here!" he whispered excitedly. "The table—the one in the picture! Mrs. Oxenstern must've bought it. It's right over there by the sofa—go ahead, see for yourself!"

Miss Eells was stunned—she had never expected a development like this. Silently she set down her cup and saucer and walked to the other end of the room. A few seconds later she was back, and her face was pale. "You're absolutely right, Anthony!" she whispered in an awestruck voice. "That's it, all right. No doubt about it. When Emerson hears the news, he'll really flip!"

Anthony glanced nervously at Mrs. Oxenstern, who was standing at the other end of the room. "Do you think she knows?" he asked. "About the Autarchs and their mansion, I mean."

Miss Eells laughed. "Are you kidding? Mrs. O. thinks the table is a valuable antique—that's why she bought it. And to tell the truth we don't really know much more than that. Emerson's idea about using the table and some playing cards to get back to the misty mansion . . . well, it may just be a lot of hogwash. At any rate, we're not going to try to smuggle the table out of here tonight. I'll give him a call later this evening and find out what he wants to do next."

The party ended, and the guests went home. Mrs. Oxenstern locked the doors and turned out the lights. But just before she went to bed she came downstairs in her bathrobe and slippers to have one more look at the antique writing desk that she had bought. She was proud of the desk, but she had to admit that there was something odd about it. It fascinated her in a way that was unsettling—almost as if it were alive. Mrs. Oxenstern turned on the living room lights. There by the grand piano stood the little desk, which had been designed by the noted Victorian architect Frank Furness. Mr. Furness usually designed buildings, but he also did a few bureaus and desks—they were quite rare. Slowly Mrs. Oxenstern crossed the room. She walked around the desk, admiring the fine leather top with its border of little gilded flowers. She ran her hand over the polished ebony rail with its knobby miniature columns and carved fan ornament at the back. Then she slid out the drawer in the front—it was empty, but there were ink stains on the bottom, and it smelled of pencil shavings. A valuable and beautiful object, but nothing more. Giving the desk an affectionate little pat, Mrs. Oxenstern glanced at it once more and then hurried off to bed.

The hours of the night slowly passed. At two in the morning the grandfather clock on the stair landing struck, and Mrs. Oxenstern suddenly sat bolt upright in her bed. It wasn't the clock that had awakened her but a noise, a noise downstairs. Mrs. Oxenstern had lived in this old house a long time, and she knew all its noises. Rattle rattle bang, rattle rattle bang. This was the sound of one of the French doors in the living room—it was loose and swinging back and forth in the wind. Maria, Mrs. Oxenstern's live-in maid, was to have locked up the house. Apparently she hadn't done a very good job, and she would hear from her employer in the morning. With a discontented sigh, Mrs. Oxenstern threw back the covers and swung herself out of bed. In slippers and bathrobe once more, she marched angrily down the carpeted steps and strode into the living room. Then she stopped and stared. One glass-paned door was swinging back and forth, and a cold wind blew into the room. The desk was surrounded by a trembling halo of gray light, and behind it stood a tall gaunt man in a black frock coat. Mrs. Oxenstern recognized him immediately—it was Mr. Ambrose, the man in the painting. She had seen it on the stair when she came to buy the desk. Now as she stood frozen in terror, she saw that the man was fingering some playing cards that lay on the desk. And she heard the words: *Three, seven, nine. And the ace of spades reversed is death!* Then the face of the man changed, so that now she saw a horrible decaying corpse, with glazed unseeing eyes and pallid lips pulled back in a rigid grin. The creature's eyes met hers, and she fell to the floor unconscious.

CHAPTER THIRTEEN

The next afternoon everyone in Hoosac was reading about Mrs. Hanson Oxenstern's encounter with a ghost in her own living room. It was quite a tale, and Mrs. Oxenstern had told it herself to a reporter from the Hoosac *News*, who showed up at her house in response to a frantic phone call. Miss Eells got the newspaper delivered to the library around four in the afternoon. She sat in her office reading the article aloud to Anthony:

"... and so Mrs. Oxenstern believes that she has seen a genuine apparition, the spirit of Mr. Ambrose, the long-dead owner of a gloomy mansion in New Stockholm, Wisconsin. A psychic from Minneapolis has volunteered to

cleanse Mrs. Oxenstern's house of evil pres-
ences, but she is not interested in such things.
She will sell the desk and a mirror that was
also the property of Mr. Ambrose, and that,
she feels, will be all that is necessary to give
her peace of mind once again."

Miss Eells put the paper down and looked up. Nor-
mally a story like this would have amused her, but she
wasn't laughing now. She knew that Mr. Ambrose was
not dead—instead he had vanished into another dimension, and he had become the evil creature known as the
Grand Autarch. But if he wasn't dead, why had his
ghostly form been seen hovering near the desk he used
to own?

"I wonder what Emerson will have to say about all
this?" said Miss Eells, as she stared absently at her clut-
tered desktop. "He's supposed to be such a big expert
on the occult, so I suppose he will have some half-baked
explanation for what happened." She looked question-
ingly at Anthony. "Do you think I should call him and
tell him?"

Anthony blinked in astonishment. "Why . . . why
wouldn't you want to tell him?" he asked.

Miss Eells frowned and bit her lip. "Because he'll want
to buy the desk, that's why!" she said vehemently. "When
I called him last night and told him my news, he immediately started making plans to break into Mrs. O.'s
house and swipe the desk. Can you imagine? He really
wants to go back to that otherworld and find the cube

before the Autarchs do." Miss Eells folded her arms and threw herself back in her chair. The chair hit a small potted plant that was perched on a shelf nearby. It fell to the floor and smashed, of course. Anthony ran to get a broom and dustpan, and soon the mess was cleaned up. But as he was putting the clay fragments and the dirt into a wastebasket, Anthony turned suddenly.

"Miss Eells, what if he's right?" he said in a trembling voice. "What if those awful people really can invade our world and change it? Maybe we ought to pay attention to what Emerson says and help him before it's too late!"

Miss Eells rolled her eyes upward and sank back disgustedly into her swivel chair. "Heavens, Anthony!" she exclaimed. "I've lived with Emerson all my life, and I know him a lot better than you do! His mind churns out weird theories the way a meat grinder grinds out meat. It's true that by accident you found a way to that frightening moonlit world. But there's no evidence that the coin with the word *wabe* scratched on it is a clue of any sort. Maybe the person who hid the coin is named Wabe—Thaddeus Q. Wabe, the well-known vandal who ruins the value of rare coins. In any case, I think that the way back to Miserable Acres is closed forever, and Mr. Ambrose's desk isn't going to fly us back there. Emerson's theory is just a lot of hooey."

Anthony looked at Miss Eells challengingly. "Well, if it's a lot of hooey," he asked, "then why don't you tell him about the desk?" Immediately Anthony regretted what he had said. He hardly ever spoke sharply to Miss Eells, but he really believed in Emerson's ideas.

At first Miss Eells was surprised by what Anthony said, but then she laughed. "Em has always told me that I don't have a logical mind," she said, still chuckling. "And this certainly proves it! All right, all right . . . I'm not being reasonable or sensible. I guess in the back of my mind I have this awful fear that my brother might be right about the magic powers of that old desk. If it can whisk him back to the misty mansion, then he may land in a heap of trouble. And what's worse, we'll probably go with him, and *we'll* be in danger too!" She paused and scratched her ear thoughtfully. "Oh, well!" she sighed at last as she glanced at the phone on her desk. "He is my dear brother and I've never hidden anything—anything important—from him in my life. Maybe when he hears what happened to Mrs. Oxenstern, he won't want the desk after all. Who knows?" And with that she picked up the receiver, dialed O, and asked the operator for long distance.

Needless to say, Emerson got very excited when he heard about what happened. And he was not at all afraid of the ghostly shape that had frightened the wits out of Mrs. Oxenstern. It was, he explained patiently, merely an astral body, a thing projected by the evil brain of Mr. Ambrose, alias the Grand Autarch.

"My amulets will protect us as they did before," said Emerson calmly. "You really shouldn't worry, sis—you'll be in good hands if you decide to come back to the mansion with me. I'll be going, and I imagine that Anthony will want to come too. We'll find that cube and smash it or bring it back with us."

"As easy as that, eh?" said Miss Eells. "Em, you are a brilliant man, but you tend to be overconfident, as I've told you at least eight thousand times in the past. Even if you can use that dratted desk to go back to that otherworld, there'll be a lot of danger. Do you understand that?"

"Of course I do!" said Emerson. "Now didn't you say that Mrs. Oxenstern was getting rid of a mirror that she got at Ambrose's house. Do you know anything about that?"

"Of course not!" Miss Eells shot back. "Why do you want to know about this mirror?"

"Because it may be important," grumbled Emerson. "Look, I'll be down to see you tomorrow morning. And when I go over to buy that desk I'm going to say that my name is Emerson Dittersdorf. If I mention the name Eells, she'll probably throw me out on my ear!"

"Probably," said Miss Eells, and with that she hung up.

The next morning, true to his word, Emerson showed up at Miss Eells's house. As usual he was driving his 1938 LaSalle, but this time a green wooden trailer was hitched to the rear bumper. Emerson was wearing a very snazzy blue pinstripe suit he had bought in London and a trench coat with lots of pockets and flaps. After having breakfast with his sister he drove over to Mrs. Oxenstern's house and rang her bell. He told Mrs. Oxenstern that he was an antique collector from St. Cloud, and he wanted to buy her rare Frank Furness desk. Needless to say, Mrs. Oxenstern was only too happy to get the desk off her hands, and she said she would throw in an antique mirror for free. Emerson paid cash for the desk; then he lugged it out to the trailer and laid it carefully on its side. The mirror was wrapped up in brown paper and tied with twine; Emerson put it on the floor of the trailer next to the desk. Then he threw a tarpaulin over everything and lashed it securely to the sides of the trailer. After a final thank-you to Mrs. Oxenstern, Emerson drove to Miss Eells's house on Pine Street. When he entered the living room he could see that she was pretty nervous.

"Emerson, you're not bringing that haunted desk into my house!" she said. "I wouldn't be able to sleep a wink if—"

"Myra!" snapped Emerson, cutting her off. "I'm just going to have a cup of tea. Then I'll drive straight back to St. Cloud with my loot. And then—"

"Oh, don't tell me, don't tell me!" exclaimed Miss Eells, waving her hands in front of her face as if to fend off her brother. "When you get home you're going to put on that Gobi desert sand amulet and wear it all the time, and that will protect you from the ghosties. Am I right?"

"You're way ahead of me," said Emerson. "Yes, that is exactly what I am going to do. And when I think the time is right I'm going to go back to find that sundial and dig near it." He paused and stared hard at Miss Eells. "And I could use some help," he added solemnly. "I really could."

"I'll think about it," she said quietly. Then she smiled. "Come on, brother," she said, as she led the way to the kitchen. "We have Lapsang Souchong tea and English muffins with strawberries and whipped cream and honey. A second breakfast before you start your long drive back to St. Cloud. Sound good?"

Emerson nodded and rubbed his hands cheerfully. Like his sister, he loved to eat.

CHAPTER FOURTEEN

During the weeks that followed, Miss Eells thought about Emerson a lot. She worried and paced the carpet during the wee hours of the morning. Because Anthony was her friend, she often told him about her fears, but if she wanted to be reassured, she was talking to the wrong person. Anthony was a real first-class worrywart, and he expected that a disaster of some sort would happen to Emerson. So they both got anxious together, which didn't help things much.

One evening Miss Eells got a phone call from Emerson. To her great relief, he seemed to be all right, though it was clear from the sound of his voice that he was discouraged. He had expected to find playing cards hidden away in some secret compartment of the desk. But there weren't any cards, and as far as Emerson could tell, there weren't any secret compartments. He had had the desk X-rayed, and there were no hollow legs; the drawer was just a drawer, with no false bottom or sliding panels. Without the cards, the desk wouldn't do anything for him—Emerson was convinced of that. And why was he so sure that he would need the cards shown in the painting? Well, he had examined the leather top of the desk, and he had found rows of pinprick holes— four rectangles were formed, one for each card. They were arranged this way:

Miss Eells was secretly overjoyed that Emerson had run into a stone wall, but she tried to be sympathetic. Then she asked him if he had seen or heard anything strange since he bought the desk.

"Of course not!" said Emerson disdainfully. "I told you these amulets of mine work—the forces of evil can't come near me as long as I wear one."

"Well, that's encouraging, I must say!" Miss Eells replied cheerfully. "By the way, how do you like the mirror? I never saw it—what's it like?"

"It's a bit odd," said Emerson. "I'd call it Victorian trash. The bottom part is pointed like a church window, and it's enclosed in a gilded wooden frame. Then up on top are three little round mirrors, also in gilt frames. The whole effect is—"

Miss Eells interrupted Emerson with a gasp—she suddenly realized that the "window" she and Anthony had seen in the painting was really a mirror! When she explained this to Emerson, he got very excited.

"Myra!" he exclaimed joyfully. "I think you've put me onto something! I'll call you back later!" and with that he hung up.

Miss Eells was thoroughly befuddled. She couldn't imagine what Emerson was thinking of, but she found out about half an hour later: He had pried loose a wooden slab that covered the back of the mirror, and there, glued to the slab, he had found the four playing cards: the ace, three, seven, and nine of spades.

"So you see, Myra, it's going to work after all!" crowed Emerson. When I put those cards in place we'll be able to return to the world of the Autarchs. I can't thank you enough for putting me on the right track!"

"Don't mention it," mumbled Miss Eells faintly. Secretly she was kicking herself for having such a big mouth. She should have kept it shut about the mirror in the painting—she really should have!

"So what are you going to do now?" asked Miss Eells warily.

"Why, I'm going back to the Autarchs' world, just as I said I would." Emerson paused, and his voice softened. He sounded gentle and coaxing, like someone who doesn't want to offend. "Won't you come with me, Myra?" he asked. "I said before that I'll need help, and I really meant it. There won't be any danger—with the amulets we'll be perfectly safe. And I could use Anthony's strong arms to help with the digging."

Miss Eells didn't know what to say. She still didn't believe that the desk and the playing cards could take them back to the Autarchs' world. But if Emerson's crazy plan really worked, they would all be at risk. She did not trust her brother's devil-may-care optimism. What should she say?

"Are you still there, Myra?" asked Emerson. He was beginning to sound impatient.

"Yes, yes!" snapped Miss Eells. "Give me some time, for heaven's sake!" She chewed her fingernails and thought some more. Finally she convinced herself that Emerson's plan couldn't possibly work. So she would volunteer to go along and bring Anthony with her. And then when they were all left standing on Emerson's living room rug, she could say that she had done her best to be loyal and helpful.

"Very well, Emerson," she said at last. "I'll go with you. So when are you planning to make this exciting trip?"

"I am planning to go this coming Saturday," he said solemnly. "Around eight in the evening, after dinner. I'll expect you and Anthony around six. How will that be?"

"I'll try," said Miss Eells, and with that she said good-bye and hung up.

When she told Anthony about what had happened he got very interested. "You mean we're really going back there?" he asked excitedly.

Miss Eells laid her hand on Anthony's arm and smiled sadly. "I know you're raring to go," she said, "but if I were you I wouldn't get my hopes up. We're just going up to Em's place to be polite."

Anthony looked disappointed. "You don't think it'll work, then?"

Miss Eells shook her head. "No, I don't. And why you two want to go back to that frightening place is more than I can figure out. Anyway, get permission from your folks to go up to St. Cloud around four on Saturday. We'll be staying overnight—after Emerson's hocus-pocus fizzles."

The rest of the week passed quickly for Anthony, and when he showed up to work at the library on Saturday morning, he had his suitcase with him. Whether or not the grand scheme worked, he always enjoyed visiting Emerson's vast Victorian house with its strange old-fashioned furniture and odd collection of magical objects. So for the rest of the day, Anthony shelved books and dusted mantels and ran the vacuum cleaner over rugs in various rooms of the library. Finally three o'clock arrived, and Miss Eells rang a little gong as she always did to announce that the place was closing. People filed out, and the front door was bolted. Anthony felt a tightening in his stomach. Miss Eells hummed cheerfully as she turned out the lights and checked the windows. Then, with her big ring of keys in her hand, she motioned for Anthony to get his suitcase and follow her to the back entrance. When the last door was locked, Anthony followed Miss Eells to her car, a lovely white Cadillac, which was a present from Emerson. They put the suitcases into the trunk and climbed into the car. Miss Eells revved up the motor. They were on their way.

Around eight that evening, Anthony and Miss Eells were sitting in Emerson's parlor. Two of the walls were covered by built-in bookcases full of rare old volumes. A large red Oriental rug lay in front of leather covered easy chairs and bronze floor lamps. Chinese vases and other knickknacks dotted the shelves and tables. In the middle of the room stood Mr. Ambrose's desk with the ugly gold-bordered mirror propped up beside it. A little stack of playing cards had been placed on one corner of the desktop. Miss Eells and Anthony sat in the easy chairs. Emerson was standing near the desk, dressed in his lumberjack outfit: red-plaid shirt, khaki trousers, and combat boots. He held a small collapsible shovel with a red blade. As the other two watched, he leaned it up against one side of the desk. Then he picked up the mirror and moved it to a corner of the room, where it would be out of the way.

"Well!" said Emerson, turning to his guests and rubbing his hands briskly. There was an expectant hush in the room. Something wonderful and frightening was going to happen—or maybe it wasn't. In any case, they'd all know pretty soon.

"Are you going to distribute the amulets?" asked Miss Eells. She tried to sound lighthearted and amused, but there was a tremble in her voice.

"Yes," said Emerson in his best businesslike manner. "I'll just fetch the box and you can choose the ones you want." He walked over to a long library table and picked up the mahogany case that he had had with him in the Canadian cottage. Opening the lid, he went to Anthony first. As before, Anthony picked the tiny Russian icon that hung from a braided gold chain. Miss Eells took the Joachimsthaler, and of course, Emerson already had his Gobi desert sand tube hanging from a leather strap around his neck. Quietly Emerson closed the lid of the box and put it back on the table. Then he strode back to the desk and bowed to his two guests.

"We're ready to go," he announced. "If you're coming with me, place your hand somewhere on one of the sides of the desk."

Anthony got up. So did Miss Eells. Emerson took his place at the desk like an orchestra conductor. On his left stood Anthony, touching the varnished side of the desk. Miss Eells stood on the right. After clearing his throat two or three times Emerson picked up the cards. First he laid the three of spades down in the place marked out for it. Next came the seven and the nine. Last of all, Emerson laid down the ace in the little dotted rectangle on the left. Nothing happened.

For quite a long time the three of them stood there dead still. Then Miss Eells jerked her hand away from the side of the desk. She felt extremely relieved, but she patted Emerson on the arm and smiled kindly. "Don't feel bad, Em," she muttered. "After all, you tried."

"Yeah," put in Anthony. "It really wasn't your fault, Mr. Eells."

Emerson had not moved a muscle. His hand still lay on the ace, and on his face was an angry and humiliated look. With a quick motion, he gathered up the cards and piled them at one corner of the desk. Then he lifted his hand and brought it down on the leather-covered surface with a loud slap. "*Blast it all!*" he exclaimed. "I thought it would work—I really did!" For several seconds he stood chewing his lip and thinking furiously. Then he turned to Miss Eells. "Tell me, Myra," he said in a commanding voice. "Where was the mirror in the painting? You know, the one you thought was a window?"

Miss Eells was startled by this question. She didn't have the faintest idea of what Emerson was driving at. "Well," she said slowly, "in the painting of Mr. Ambrose the mirror—the one that looked like a window— it was . . . was . . ."

"Yes?" said Emerson impatiently. "It was where?"

"Oh, give me time for heaven's sake!" exclaimed Miss

Eells in exasperation. "The mirror was up over Mr. Ambrose's left shoulder."

"That's all I need to know," said Emerson. "Anthony, help me move the desk back toward that wall over there."

Throwing the shovel to one side for the time being, Emerson helped Anthony lug the desk over to a nearby wall where a painting hung. Emerson took down the painting and put the mirror up in its place. Then he walked back to the middle of the room and picked up the shovel. Once again he propped it against the desk.

"Places everyone!" he said in a commanding voice. "Myra, Anthony, go stand where you were before with your hands on the desk. We're going to have another try."

As soon as the other two were in place Emerson picked up the cards and glanced quickly over his left shoulder. Then he lifted the three of spades in the air and put it down on the desk. Immediately the mirror began to glow with a grayish light that cast a shimmering halo around the three people who stood at the desk. A drumming sound began under the floor of the room. At this point Miss Eells would have jerked her hand away from the side of the desk, but she found that she couldn't. Emerson laid down the seven and the nine. The light got brighter, and the drumming got louder. A vase on the library table rocked and then crashed to the floor, and several books fell out of a bookcase. Still remaining calm,

Emerson lifted the ace dramatically in the air. He held it upside down, the same position shown in the painting. But as Emerson was about to lay the card down, Anthony let out a loud exclamation.

"Don't, Mr. Eells! Don't lay it down! It's a trap!"

Emerson was startled. With the card still held in the air he turned to Anthony. "For heaven's sake, why not?" he asked.

"Because the ace of spades upside down is *death!*" Anthony cried desperately. "I read about it in a book somewhere! We'll all die if you put the card down like that!"

Emerson wondered: Were they being set up for death by the evil Mr. Ambrose? After another moment of hesitation Emerson turned the card around so that the big spade symbol and the word *bicycle* were right side up facing him. Carefully he laid the card down.

All of a sudden a lot of things happened. The walls and floor of the room seemed to waver, and the bookcases and paintings sagged. The drumming noise grew to a deafening roar, as the blue light became a blinding glare. Then the three people who were standing at the desk were whirled round and round, as if they were standing on some large spinning turntable. Faster and faster they spun, and just before he blacked out Anthony heard himself yelling, *"We're gonna die anyway! Oh no. . . ."*

CHAPTER FIFTEEN

When Miss Eells, Anthony, and Emerson came to, they felt very dizzy and scared to death. As before they were grouped around the desk, but they weren't in Emerson's parlor anymore. They were in a gloomy vaulted chamber that seemed to be a crypt. All around them they saw deep niches set in the rough stone walls, and many of these held coffins. Low gray arches supported the ceiling, and rows of squat pillars marched away into the distance. The place smelled damp and moldy and the still air seemed clammy, bone-chilling, and somehow evil. Emerson shuddered and wiped his face with his handkerchief.

"Well, here we are—wherever that is!" he announced, as he peered around at the grim scene. "Probably we are in some part of the black stone mansion of the Autarchs. We have to go outside to search for the sundial."

Miss Eells was just recovering from the shock of the whirling journey they had been on. Once again she silently accused herself: If she had not gone along with Emerson's plans, she wouldn't be here. But there was no turning back now.

Emerson picked up the four playing cards and put them in his hip pocket. Then, after grabbing the shovel, he began to walk down the corridor. Miss Eells and Anthony followed him past the stone arches. The chamber was lit by a grayish glow that seemed to come from nowhere in particular. At last they arrived at a stone staircase that spiraled upward into shadows. But as they were about to start climbing, someone came bounding down the steps to meet them. He was a short, elderly man with a wrinkly face and sagging cheeks. Bare feet peeked out of the folds of his tattered black robe and straggly gray hair hung down over his hunched shoulders. But in spite of his shabby appearance and the frightening way he had jumped out at them, the three travelers somehow knew that they had nothing to fear from this man. There was an air of kindness and gentleness about him, and his mouth was pursed up into a wistful pout.

"Oh, hello there!" said the little man, waving shyly. "Imagine meeting you folks here!"

Anthony, Emerson, and Miss Eells had been startled

at first, but now they were merely curious. Who was this man, and why was he acting as if he knew who they were?

Emerson thought a bit. He had a hunch that he knew who this was, but he couldn't be sure yet. Holding out his hand he smiled politely and said, "Emerson Eells at your service! And who, pray tell, might you be?"

The little man giggled. "I'll bet you know already," he exclaimed. "My name is Wabe. Nathaniel Wabe, formerly of the grand society of Autarchs. Pleased to meet you all!"

Anthony was stunned, but then his heart sank. This had to be the man who had scratched WABE on the gold coin. But because that was his name was the clue meaningless? Had they come all this way for nothing?

"In case you were wondering," the man went on, "I'm the one who left the note in the vase in your cottage. I used to make lots of trips back and forth between this world and Earth, but I don't get around much anymore. I became frightened after three people from your world found my note and came here. Unfortunately they were caught and now they're decorating the garden outside. After that happened, I began to realize the true wickedness of what was going on here, and I hid the Logos Cube. Needless to say, I had to hide *myself* after that, and ever since then I've been living in the secret passages of this mansion, like a rat in a maze. I know ways of getting around that even the Grand Autarch doesn't know, and I've stayed alive by raiding the kitchen at odd hours. Even Autarchs have to munch, you know." He giggled again in a very disconcerting way.

Anthony's head was whirling. This was the man who had started them on their quest! There were a million questions that he wanted to ask, but he asked the one that seemed most important. "Mr. . . . Mr. Wabe," he stammered, "if your name really is Wabe, then is the clue . . . I mean, the word, is it . . ."

"Is it all just a joke, then?" asked the little man, reading his thoughts. "Of course not! When I lived in Eau Claire, Wisconsin, I used to read a lot, and I know a lot of poems by heart. One of them is *Jabberwocky*. And I always thought how strange it was that one of the nonsense words in the poem was my last name. So I decided to give the word a little—uh, shall we say—added significance?"

Emerson beamed—his theory had been right, then! "Are we to understand that the Logos Cube is buried near a sundial?" he asked eagerly.

The little man laughed and shook his head. "Oh, dear me, no! You've got it all wrong! What I buried is something you need to *destroy* the cube! It's no good having the cube if you don't possess the thing that can get rid of it."

Emerson looked puzzled. "But I don't understand," he said. "If you have the thing that will shatter the cube, why in heaven's name don't you use it?"

The little man sighed. "I can't. Long ago I took a blood oath to protect the cube, and an Autarch's oath has a magical effect on him. I couldn't raise my hand to damage the cube in any way—the weapon would fall from my hand. So I just hid the wretched thing away and tried to provide someone else with the means of getting rid of it."

"I see," said Emerson, scratching his head uncertainly. "Well, in that case why don't you tell us where the cube is? We can take it to the place where the weapon is hidden and smash it there. Or if we can't destroy it we can at least carry it back to Minnesota with us. Doesn't that make sense?"

The man smiled sheepishly. "It would," he said, "except for one small problem: I don't remember where I put it."

Emerson's mouth dropped open. "You . . . you *what?*" he spluttered.

"I said, I don't remember where it is," the man explained patiently. "You see, when I swiped the cube I made the mistake of staring at it too long, and it addled my brain. I've been in hiding for several years, and that doesn't improve your memory. There is a clue inscribed on the weapon that you must use, but I don't remember what it is. Besides, the weapon is buried outside, and I can't go outside for fear of getting caught."

"Oh, great!" muttered Emerson. He chewed his lip. What should he do next? "Well," he said at last, "can you at least show us a way of getting out of here? I assume that the weapon is buried in that garden—am I right?"

"Oh, yes, absolutely!" replied the little man, nodding eagerly. "As for getting out of here, I think I remember a way . . . if it's still there."

Emerson blinked and stared at the man. To him it seemed that things were getting more confused by the minute. "What do you mean by *that?*" asked Emerson. "Has someone blocked up the way?"

"No, no, no!" said the little man, shaking his head vigorously. "I don't mean that at all!" He heaved a sad sigh and sat down on one of the stone steps. "Let me try to make something clear to you," he went on gloomily. "Lately the Logos Cube has gone wild. At first it just did little odd, annoying things, like changing the pictures on walls or the color of flowers in vases. But then rooms began to vanish and passageways were suddenly blocked. Windows were breaking in the night for no reason at all. And when I was eavesdropping on the kitchen help the other day, I heard that one of the Autarchs had vanished!" He chuckled unpleasantly. "Lord knows where he is! The Cube may have sent him off to another dimension, or it may simply have vaporized him. It has a will of its own now, like a rebellious robot or a thinking machine that has gone mad. I'm just trying to warn you about what you'll be up against when you try to get out of this place."

Silence fell. Suddenly Miss Eells reached out and

tugged at Emerson's coatsleeve. "For the love of Pete, Em!" she whispered hoarsely, "let's go back to that desk and get out of here! We're liable to get killed looking for the thing to smash the cube! What are we waiting for?"

Emerson hesitated. For once he thought that his sister might be right. They had landed in a situation that was much more dangerous than it had seemed. But just as Emerson was turning to lead the way back, a loud crash startled everyone. A stone wall suddenly appeared in the middle of the vaulted chamber—the way back to the desk was blocked.

Emerson turned to Miss Eells and grimaced. "Any other suggestions?" he said quietly.

Anthony felt his stomach churning. Were they trapped forever in this frightening world? But when he looked at Emerson he saw the determined look on his face and the glitter in his eyes, and he knew that good old Em would not give up without a fight.

"We'll go up these steps and see where they lead!" said Emerson, setting his jaw with determination. He turned back toward the stairs, and he half expected to see that Nathaniel Wabe had vanished. But there he was, sitting calmly with a silly smile on his face.

"You see what I mean?" said the little man, with a helpless shrug. "The cube is liable to do anything, at any time. But if you want to find a way to the outside, I might be able to help you."

Deciding that bad help was better than no help at all, Emerson sighed and told him to lead on. They walked up the stairs till they came to a broad corridor that stretched in both directions. The walls of the corridor were covered with red velvet and fancy brass wall sconces. Stepping onto the polished hardwood surface, Emerson motioned for Anthony and Miss Eells to follow. Nathaniel started to lead them to the right, but he had not taken many steps when a hole opened in the floor in front of him, and with a loud cry he vanished from sight. The floor closed over him, and silence returned.

Horrified, Anthony and his friends stared at the place where Nathaniel had been. Now they were really frightened; they were on their own in this treacherous ever-changing place. Suddenly Anthony panicked. With a loud yell he ran to the left. The others ran after him, calling for him to stop. Anthony skidded around a corner and was horrified by what was taking place in the room before him: Silver candlesticks were changing into wormy wooden logs, and the framed paintings on the wall were going blank. A long walnut table turned to rubber and collapsed. Silver bowls flew into the air and popped like soap bubbles. Chairs chased each other on carved knobby legs, and a bust of a Roman emperor turned to a melting wax horror. Nothing seemed solid—would the floor give way next? In fear Anthony stepped back, but as he turned to retrace his steps he found that a blank wall of granite blocks had slid into place, barring his way. He was alone.

CHAPTER SIXTEEN

Meanwhile, Emerson and Miss Eells stood staring help-lessly at the stone wall that had unexpectedly cut them off from their friend. In anger Emerson raised his shovel and banged at the blocks with it. The blade rebounded from the hard granite with a loud *dinggg!* and Emerson turned away in disgust.

"I was hoping the wall would turn out to be an illu-sion," he muttered. "But as you see it's solid!" Tears came to Emerson's eyes. It was all his fault. He had led his sister and Anthony on this wild-goose chase. He had been so sure that he could smash the cube and get home without any serious problems. And now where were they? All three of them would probably die for nothing, with their mission unaccomplished.

As Emerson stood there fighting the urge to cry he felt Miss Eells's soft touch on his arm. "Don't worry, Em," she said quietly. "We'll get out of this. Walls that suddenly appear can vanish. Somehow we'll all get back together and go home. I'm sure of it."

Emerson smiled weakly. He took off his glasses, dabbed at his eyes with his handkerchief, and put the glasses on again. "Thanks, Sis," he said in a voice thick with emotion. Then with a shuddering sigh Emerson pulled himself together. Once more he was the brave, indomitable leader—at least he hoped that he was.

"Now, then!" said Emerson, setting his jaw purposefully. "We'll have to go down this hall. It's the only way left to us. Somewhere there has to be a passage leading to the outdoors. Come on."

Emerson and Miss Eells marched down the corridor, their footsteps echoing on the hardwood floors. Doors opened and closed on either side of them, and in the rooms they saw objects whiz by and furniture change into all sorts of unlikely things. Finally they came to a door which was firmly closed. Large gold Gothic letters announced: COUNCIL ROOM.

Emerson halted and grabbed Miss Eells's arm. "Wait!" he said as he turned toward the door with sudden interest. "This is the room that Anthony and I spied on. Somewhere in there is the peephole we used, and behind that is the secret passage that leads outside. It's worth a try."

Seizing the knob firmly, Emerson opened the door.

Inside the room everything was quiet and orderly. Apparently the Autarchs' magic was still powerful here, in spite of what the cube was doing elsewhere. The long polished table with empty chairs and the ornate cushioned throne that the Grand Autarch sat in were undisturbed. A gilded eighteenth-century clock ticked quietly on the mantel of the marble fireplace, as if everything in the world was going along fine. Brown tapestries hung on the walls; they showed horrible scenes of battle from the Middle Ages.

"Over there!" said Emerson, pointing at a tapestry on the far wall. "We were looking into the room from that direction, so the passage must be behind that wall." Walking quickly across the room, Emerson stooped and examined a soldier who lay stretched out on the embroidered ground. One of the buttons of his jacket was missing, and the hole where the button should have been was the peephole.

"Ah-*hah!*" crowed Emerson, hauling Miss Eells forward so she could see what he was pointing at. "There it is! I was right!"

"Yes, I see it!" exclaimed Miss Eells. "You've found the peephole—what do we do next?"

Without a word Emerson walked to the corner of the tapestry and raised it. Behind the heavy dusty hanging was varnished wood paneling. A thin line separated one set of panels from the next, and Emerson began to edge his way along behind the tapestry, testing for openings. Finally he found a knothole plugged with putty. Pushing at it, he tripped a hidden spring and a section of paneling moved inward—he had found the door.

"I've found it!" Emerson's muffled voice rang out from behind the tapestry. Hastily Miss Eells ran around to join him, but the dust on the tapestry got into her nose and made her sneeze violently several times. It was quite awhile before she recovered. "So here we are!" she muttered as she blew her nose. "It's dark back here. Did you bring a flashlight with you?"

Emerson reached into the right pocket of his shirt—his St. Christopher Pen-Lite was supposed to be there. But it wasn't. Emerson remembered that he had been showing it to Anthony after dinner. Anthony had probably absentmindedly stuck it in his own pocket. Cursing quietly, Emerson felt in his left pocket. There was a box of England's Glory matches, which he used to light his pipe. Emerson handed the box to his sister.

"This is the best I can do, I'm afraid," he said, as he pressed the matches into her hand. "Just keep lighting them as long as you can."

Miss Eells struck the big wooden matches one after another as they made their way along the carpeted passage. The stuffy air was filled with the smell of burned matches, and a few times Miss Eells let a match burn till it singed her fingers. Then she would yell "Ow!" drop the match, and light another. Strange, loud noises could be heard on the other side of the walls, and sometimes the floor groaned under their feet. The place was coming apart, there was no doubt about that. Could they get out before the ceiling fell in on their heads?

At last Emerson and Miss Eells came to the end of the passage. By the light of a fizzling match they saw a stone slab set in a corniced arch.

"You were here before!" whispered Miss Eells. "How does this thing open?"

"From the inside, easy as pie!" Emerson answered, and he reached out to give the slab a light push. Noiselessly it swung open, and they stepped forth into the gray moonlit world that lay beyond the mansion. In the distance was the garden with its writhing stone figures and the eerie hanging wall of glowing mist. And near a thornbush that grew against the mansion's wall stood the Grand Autarch. His arms were folded, and a grim look of triumph lit his evil face.

"Greetings!" said the Autarch in his harsh, grating voice. "Have you been enjoying yourselves?"

Emerson's blood froze, and he stepped backward. Frantically Miss Eells clutched his arm, squeezing it tight. "How . . . how did you know we were here?" asked Emerson in a weak voice. It seemed like a stupid thing to say, but it was all that came to his mind.

"I have powers of telepathy here in this world," the Autarch answered. "And other powers too, as you will presently find out. I sensed that you were here as soon as you arrived, but I wasn't sure exactly where in the mansion you might be. So I guessed that you had somehow managed to locate this old passage again."

"*Again?*" said Emerson, his eyes wide with astonishment. "You mean—"

"Yes, indeed," snapped the Autarch, cutting him off. "When you were here the last time, you trampled down the grass outside the passage's entrance, and because no one here uses the passage anymore, I knew that you had done it. How did you get back to my world? When I smashed that purple window, I thought I had spoiled your fun for good!"

"We used your desk," said Emerson with a grim smile. Even if they were going to die he wanted the Autarch to know that they had solved one of his clever riddles.

"My desk!" said the Autarch, grinning unpleasantly. "Ah, yes! When I first created this house—with the help of my friends, of course—I used the desk to take me back and forth. How very brilliant of you to work out its secrets and avoid the death trap too! I must congratulate you, Mr. Eells. But I have a nasty, vengeful nature, and I haven't forgotten the beating you gave me when I visited your cottage. Soon you and your dear sister will be smothered in statues of living stone. But first I need some information from you. *Where is the Logos Cube?*"

Emerson was totally stunned by this question. He couldn't have been more surprised if the Autarch had asked him for a piece of the moon on a platter. With all his powers of telepathy the Grand Autarch had things wrong! Maybe the amulet of Gobi desert sand was protecting the inner recesses of Emerson's mind, or maybe it was his native stubbornness that saved him—whatever the reason was, Emerson was grateful. His brain raced madly—what should he say? Not the truth, that was for certain. But what? Suddenly he had an inspiration—he knew what he ought to say.

"Well?" snapped the Autarch impatiently. "Out with it! Where is the cube?"

Emerson took a deep breath and let it out. "It's buried near the sundial in your garden. Mr. Wabe told me. Please—it's the truth, I swear!"

"It had better be," muttered the Autarch with an evil grimace. "If you are playing games with me, you'll wish you had never been born! I know where the sundial is. You can use that shovel to dig up the cube for me. Come!"

Emerson did his best to snivel and look totally beaten. Together, he and Miss Eells followed the Autarch into the garden of snaky vines. The vines writhed and hissed, but the outstretched hand of their master calmed them. The grim little procession passed the statues of frozen horror and came at last to the sundial in the center of the garden. The greenish-bronze dial stood on a fluted stone column, and around its edge these words were inscribed: LIFE IS A DREAM. Immediately Emerson began digging. Clods of grassy earth flew in all directions. But he was digging in the wrong place, and his work was all in vain.

"*Well?*" snapped the Autarch, tapping his foot on the gravel path. "Have you found it yet?"

"Give me time! Give me time!" panted Emerson,

wiping his sweaty forehead with his sleeve. "I haven't found it yet, but I will!"

"My patience is limited," said the Autarch ominously. "But I will give you a few more minutes—use them wisely!"

"Yes, sir!" mumbled Emerson. He looked around wildly. On the other side of the sundial was a small depression in the ground. "Oh, how stupid of me!" he said. "I've been digging in the wrong place! I'd like to try over there, if I might."

The Autarch nodded curtly, and Emerson scrambled over to the other side of the sundial and began digging again. Before long the tip of his shovel hit something that made a loud metallic *clangg*! Scrabbling madly in the dirt with his fingers, Emerson came up with . . . a hammer. It was made of some dull gray metal, and on the handle words were engraved:

> Fling me into the upper air
> I'll find the cube be it here or there!

Emerson heard gravel crunch, and he looked up to see the Grand Autarch glaring down at him. "That is not the Cube!" he growled. "What sort of game are you playing? Give it to me, whatever it is—*now!*"

With a sudden motion, Emerson leapt to his feet with the hammer in his hand. He flourished it before the startled eyes of the Autarch, and then he heaved the thing into the air. With a power of its own, the hammer soared upward and was lost in the murky leaden sky above them. Emerson and Miss Eells stared up, hoping for . . . for what? They really didn't know. From far away came a soft clink! The hammer had landed, but had its mission succeeded or failed?

CHAPTER SEVENTEEN

After the stone wall slid into place and cut him off from his friends, Anthony's panic turned into hysteria. He ran madly down the corridor till he came to a skidding halt at the foot of a staircase. Without knowing why he did this, he began to race up the steps. Anthony was a strong boy, and he could climb for a long time without getting tired. But after he had gone up two flights he paused to rest.

Ahead of him the circular stairway suddenly burst into raging flames.

Anthony gasped and nearly fell backward. He turned to run, but then he remembered that he had passed no doors. He was trapped, and the blaze was roaring toward him. He realized that his only chance was to dash right through the fire—if he could get to the other side at all. He closed his eyes tightly and pounded up the stairway.

To his surprise he felt no heat. He risked opening his eyes. He stood in the middle of billowing orange flames and boiling, oily black smoke. Then, as suddenly as it had started, the fire was gone, leaving the stairway and Anthony unsinged. The savage flames had been an illusion of some kind. Anthony swallowed and thought hard. This stairway seemed *different* to him somehow, not like the rest of the mansion. It had a more solid feel to it, as if it might lead to safety. What if the fire illusion had been intended to keep him from climbing the stairs? It seemed like the only answer, and anyway, Anthony knew there was no escape below. He would have to continue to the top.

Anthony bounded on, taking the steps two at a time. Finally, with an aching side and with sweat pouring down his face, he stumbled out through a doorway and found that he was on the roof of the mansion. Around him lay a vast lead-covered expanse, with grotesque ornaments and chimneys rising here and there. One chimney loomed directly in front of Anthony, and set in its side was an elaborate terra-cotta ornament in the shape of a howling dragon. Wedged in the dragon's gaping mouth was a small glass cube.

Instantly Anthony knew what he was looking at— this was the Logos Cube, the object the Autarchs had been searching for. It was the enchanted heart of their kingdom, and as Anthony watched, it glowed and faded, pulsing and sending forth power. The side facing him showed shifting scenes: ancient ruins amid sand dunes, forests where strange monsters roamed, and a moonlit view of a ruined chapel surrounded by black skeletal trees. Anthony watched, fascinated. He almost felt as if he could enter these strange worlds. In fact, a vague terror began to grow inside him, a fear that the cube might draw him inside it, into one of the weird scenes it showed. In spite of this queasy feeling, Anthony went on staring—he could not tear himself away.

Suddenly Anthony became aware of a figure in the distance, on the far side of the flat roof. Anthony saw him just from the corner of his eye. It was a thin, white-haired man, and he was shouting. With an effort Anthony ripped his gaze away from the cube. The figure in the distance was Emerson, and his pleading voice was hoarse with terror: "Help! Help, Anthony! They've got her! You have to save her!"

Anthony's heart leapt into his throat. The Autarchs had Miss Eells! With a gasp he stumbled across the roof, trying to reach Emerson. It was all like a horrible nightmare. The lead tiles softened and became like thick mud sucking at Anthony's feet, so that he could run only in slow motion. Even worse, the more Anthony tried to move forward, the farther away Emerson appeared to be. Emerson's voice cracked to a thin, meaningless wail, as if he had lost his mind. With hands crooked like claws, Emerson beckoned desperately, and Anthony ran even harder. At last, after what felt like an hour of effort, he saw that he was gaining. Emerson's face wrenched itself into a miserable mask of despair. Beyond him Anthony glimpsed something white and waist-high. It was a sundial on a fluted pillar. It reminded him of something, but what was it? He couldn't for the life of him remember.

"Now!" Emerson shouted. "Jump! Jump, or they'll destroy her! Jump, Anthony, jump!"

Anthony leapt, but something smacked him hard in the stomach and wrapped around him, clinging tight. "No!" shouted a high, piping voice right in his ear. "Close your eyes! Close them!"

Anthony blinked, pressed his eyelids closed, and then opened them again. Emerson and the part of the roof he had been standing on had vanished. Anthony gasped. He was hanging in space over the edge of the mansion's roof, and nothing but air was between him and the ground forty feet below. Someone's trembling arm held him and kept him from falling. "You'll have to help," whined the voice in his ear. "Once I had the strength to haul you back, but no more."

As his head cleared, Anthony found that his ankles had snagged on the edge of a low parapet. He struggled back, and whoever had caught him pulled him upright. Anthony turned and stood shaking as he faced an old, old man with bleary eyes and a hooked nose. The aged creature groaned as he released his hold. "See what they did to me," he wailed. His arms and legs began to twitch as if he were a puppet jerked this way and that on strings.

But he shrieked out an angry warning: "I was a young man, and see what they've made of me! But I'll get my revenge! I'll keep them from taking any more victims! Don't look into the cube, boy! It will scramble your brains. I looked. I looked, and see what they've done to me—no! *Don't make me! No!*"

Before Anthony could move or even cry out, the ancient man lurched forward and leapt over the parapet. Anthony flinched, expecting to hear the crunch of a body landing in the courtyard below, but that sound never came. After a moment, he took a deep breath and looked over the edge of the roof. A gray cloud hung in the air between the roof and the ground, and it was already melting away. The old man was no more. His body had simply disintegrated into mist. *That could have been me*, Anthony thought. He groped for the amulet that hung around his neck, and his fingers closed on the icon. *I have to help my friends. But how can I do it? How . . .*

He realized that he had turned his back on the cube. Without looking, he knew it was still there. He *felt* it trying furiously to make him turn and gaze into it. He had to destroy the cube somehow. How, though? If he so much as glimpsed it, the devilish thing would capture him in a web of illusion and madness—

"*What can I do?*" he yelled in despair. "*Somebody tell me what to do!*"

And then he heard a clink. Looking down he saw that a small hammer had landed on the edge of the roof. Its head was bulbous and reminded Anthony of a barrel.

The handle was of lead-colored metal, with some words inscribed on it. But before Anthony could read them, they vanished. As Anthony was staring, he heard a man's voice, very faint: "Did someone ask for advice?"

Anthony recognized the voice. It was that of Nathaniel Wabe, and it sounded as if it came from his amulet. "Yes!" Anthony said. "I need help!"

"Dear me," the voice said. "I am not quite sure where I am at the moment. I *appear* to be in an underground room or vault of some kind, all alone. Where are you?"

"On the roof!" Anthony shouted. "I'm all alone too, except for that cube and a weird-looking hammer!"

"The hammer? The hammer, did you say?" Nathaniel Wabe sounded excited. "Pick it up! Use it to smash the cube! But be very careful—don't allow the cube to capture you. It can overpower your will and make you its slave!"

Anthony let go of the amulet, and the voice faded. He reached for the hammer and closed his hand around the handle. It was like grabbing someone's arm—the shaft throbbed with life. With his other hand, Anthony clutched the amulet again. "I've got the hammer!" he shouted.

But this time there was no answer. Anthony realized he was on his own. Gathering all his strength he turned and ran toward the dragon ornament, raising the hammer high to strike. He could not help looking at the cube as he ran. It flashed brightly, so brightly that it blinded Anthony for a second.

He stumbled and fell to his knees. Somehow he did not lose his grip on the hammer. The lead roofing tiles had vanished, he realized. He was sprawled on cement. Shivering, Anthony rose and discovered that some invisible force had yanked him into a terrifying, dark, and sinister scene. He stood on the sidewalk outside Greenwood Cemetery in his hometown of Hoosac. Beyond a tall iron fence, rows of headstones marched off into the distance. It was night, and cars were crawling past on the street to Anthony's left. He wanted desperately to rush out into the street and pound on windshields and scream for help, but he couldn't do this. He was in the grip of a will more powerful than his own, and he had to obey it. Stiffly, he walked past the rows of spear-tipped iron bars till he came to the tall stone gateway. It was done in the Egyptian style, with a rayed sun on the lintel and columns carved to look like the lotus flower and its clustered stems.

In through the gate Anthony walked and down the crunching gravel drive. The hammer in his right hand steadily grew heavier and heavier, but he fought to keep his fingers locked around its handle. Wind hissed through the tall grass and the wildflowers that grew nearby as the hum of traffic grew fainter and fainter. On Anthony walked. He saw an eerie grayish glow coming from a hollow that lay beyond a little rise in the road. Anthony walked faster, and at the top of the rise he paused.

Below him lay a fearful scene. Rows of open graves stretched to the horizon, and in each grave a withered corpse sat upright in its coffin, a lighted candle in its hand. Old ladies—witches maybe—danced on a low hill nearby, and on a table-shaped stone sat a strange monstrous creature who played the bagpipes. Horns sprouted from his head, and he wore a goatish beard. From the waist down, his flanks were covered with hair, and his feet were cloven, the feet of a beast. On the creature's face was a ghastly smile, and his eyes glowed red under bushy eyebrows.

Standing dead still as if he had turned to stone, Anthony watched the grim scene. He wanted to run, but he couldn't. Every hair on his head tingled, and a chilly breath of fear ran through his body. With horror he saw that one of the witches had noticed him. She stopped dancing and let out a loud screech. The bagpipe music died with a wail, and before Anthony knew what was happening ghastly foul-smelling hags surrounded him. They poked at him and laughed shrilly. Unseen hands seized his arms in a steely grip, and they rushed him forward to the edge of a grave gouged into the raw earth. A witch thrust her nightmarish face close to his, and she tapped the face of a large watch with a bony finger.

"Want to know what time it is, sweetie?" she rasped.

Anthony couldn't answer. His lips felt stuck together, as if soldered.

A pause. Then the witch cackled and swung the watch on its gold chain. *"Time's up!"* she screeched. "If you don't know the truth, you must pay the consequences! *It's time to die!"*

A coffin appeared out of nowhere, and the unseen hands tried to wrestle Anthony into it. But the hunger to stay alive was strong in him, and he struggled violently. His right hand, still gripping the hammer, swung in an arc, and with a gasp the evil creatures fell back, freeing his left arm. With his left hand, Anthony reached inside his shirt and clutched the holy icon. Clutched it for dear life.

"Now!" he heard Nathaniel Wabe's thin voice cry. "Now while you have strength! Cry *veritas* and look into the cube!"

"*Veritas!*" Anthony shouted without thinking. As he screamed out the Latin word for *truth*, the graveyard scene vanished away, and he was on the leaded roof again. Before him was the cube—but for a moment its light flickered uncertainly. Then he saw a new scene: Emerson and Miss Eells standing on two stone pedestals in the garden near the mansion. The snaky vines had wrapped themselves around his friends' feet, and the Grand Autarch hovered nearby, surrounded by the other black-robed members of his evil society. They all raised their hands in the air, and from far away came the sound of chanting. Anthony didn't understand the words, but he knew what was happening. This time he knew it was all too real. And he knew what he had to do.

Anthony raised the hammer to strike. The scene faded. The cube was resisting him, sending forth power. The hammer trembled in his fist. The chanting of the Autarchs rose and fell like the droning of a hive of bees.

Anthony felt tremendous anger welling up inside him. With a shout he reared back, brought the hammer down, and the cube shattered.

The mansion trembled, and then it began to *dissolve*. The chimneys turned to lazy curls of red mist, and the roof became mushy. Anthony stumbled and floundered for balance. "This way! This way!" someone called out. It was Nathaniel Wabe, in the flesh. The little man stood beside a tower with an open doorway in it, and he beckoned urgently. Anthony staggered and lurched and crawled over to him. "The tower was already here when the Autarchs arrived," Wabe said. "It won't evaporate!"

The two of them reeled inside as the rest of the mansion gave a horrible gurgling sigh and billowed away as mist. Wabe seized Anthony's wrist—Anthony realized with a shock that the hammer had shattered along with the cube—and led him down a long spiral stair. At the bottom they stepped out into a clearing. The mists were drifting away, and the two of them stood on a broad moonlit island of grass and trees in the middle of nowhere. A round lake was in the center of the island, and from the shore of the lake Emerson and Miss Eells appeared, running toward them.

Joyfully Anthony called to them, and they yelled back. Anthony and Nathaniel crossed the place where the mansion had been, and there in a shallow depression stood the magic desk. They all met beside it, with Emerson and Miss Eells laughing and embracing Anthony, and Nathaniel, standing shyly to one side.

"Well," Emerson said, wiping his eyes, "I must say, I thought we were goners. They had us surrounded, and they were chanting their awful magic spell. Then just as I felt myself turning stony I saw a great flash of light, and the mansion started to billow away. About a half-second later all those black-robed maniacs simply dissolved into mist too. Which reminds me," he said, turning to Nathaniel, "why are *you* still among the solid and the living?"

With a shrug Wabe said, "Well, it's true that I cooperated in making the cube, but I never felt easy using it, don't you know. So I didn't completely surrender my will to its power. The others created the mansion and all their selfish luxuries with the cube, and so they came thoroughly under its spell. They were the creatures of the cube to such a degree that when it vanished, *they* vanished too."

Miss Eells glared at Wabe. The Autarchs had frightened her almost out of her wits when they began their chant, and now she was angry. "You talk about them as if they were never your friends," she said. "But you helped create that wretched cube, so you're partly to blame for every appalling thing that happened."

A tear trickled down Wabe's cheek, and he hung his head. "That's true. I'll never forgive myself. I'm afraid they misled me, though I let them. All I ever wanted was a place where I could be all alone and grow my vegetables and think about life. All *they* wanted was to rule the world. Silly notion, really . . . all the crowds, all the people." Wabe shuddered.

Emerson reached into his pocket for the four cards. "Well, now you can come back to Earth with us and grow your garden there."

The little old man looked forlorn and distressed. He stood wringing his hands. "Must I?"

"Why," Miss Eells said, "what else can you do? Won't this place all dissolve into mist?"

"No!" Wabe said eagerly. Only the parts that the Autarchs created with the cube. It's a little universe, you see, with nothing in it except the meadow and the woods and the lake. It's quite cozy, really, just big enough for one person. Leave me here, and I can live in the tower and tend my garden—the gardening tools and the Temple of the Winds were here when the Autarchs came, so they will endure. All my magic has vanished with the cube, and I'm quite harmless, and if you take me back to crowded, noisy Earth, I—I'm sure I'll be miserable." He began to sniffle.

"Well," Emerson said decisively, "*we* are going back. You do what you wish."

Timidly, Wabe murmured, "Perhaps you might send the desk back to me? *I* certainly don't want to rule the world, and I don't even want to have much to do with it. Only, there are a few things that I miss terribly here. Perhaps if I sent the desk to you once or twice a year you could keep me supplied with them?"

"What are they?" Emerson asked suspiciously.

"Well, Corona cigars, for one," said Wabe dreamily. "And the Sunday funny papers. And some carrot seeds. I have all the other seeds I need, but I would really love to grow some carrots."

"All right," Emerson sighed. "I suppose carrots won't be too dangerous. Ready, now?" As Anthony and Miss Eells gripped the desk, Emerson quickly laid the cards down. The spinning journey began again. Once more they all blacked out, and when they came to, they were back in Emerson's comfortable book-lined parlor.

Anthony wiped his face with his sleeve. He had never been so glad to see a place in his life. Miss Eells and Emerson were grinning from ear to ear. As Anthony and Miss Eells hugged each other, Emerson ran from the room. He was back in a few minutes with a thick stack of newspapers, a box of cigars (Dutch Masters, though, not Coronas), and a bunch of carrots. "These will have to do until I can buy some seeds for our friend," he said, opening drawers and stuffing his burdens inside. He shoved the drawers closed, dealt the cards again, and leapt back. The desk vanished away.

"I hope that was a wise thing to do, Em," Miss Eells said with a sigh. "What if Nathaniel Wabe should change his mind about wanting to rule the world? Grand Autarch Ambrose may just be a puff of mist in the wind, but if old Nathaniel decides to become Super Supreme Almighty Pooh-Bah Wabe, what's to stop him?"

"I'm sure we can trust him," Emerson said. "He's a

real hermit, and I believe that he's right about all his magic being used up. But tell us what happened, Anthony! How did you get up on the roof? And did you use the hammer?"

Anthony told the tale, starting with the panic he had felt when the stone wall blocked the hallway. When he had finished, Emerson laughed and shook his hand.

"Well done, my boy, well done! An icon that worked like Dick Tracy's two-way wrist radio! Hard to believe! But in the Autarchs' world it would fit right in, wouldn't it?" He paused. "Well, should we leave that blasted mirror where it is? If we smash it, then we will make Mr. Wabe a hermit for good and all."

"You certainly are getting destructive in your old age," said Miss Eells in a taunting voice. "I thought that was *my* routine!"

After a moment's hesitation Anthony said, "Please don't break the mirror. I mean, Mr. Wabe *did* get me off the roof of that mansion before it dissolved under my feet."

"All right," Emerson said with a scowl. "I'll leave it alone for the time being. But if the ghost of old Ambrose ever shows up, I'll turn the mirror over to my sister. She'll shatter it to smithereens without even trying!"

"Oh, Em," Miss Eells grumped. "I'm not *that* clumsy."

Emerson laughed. "Oh, no? Tell me, Myra: Did you ever smash anything on *purpose*?"

Miss Eells thought a minute. "No," she said slowly.

"I don't believe I ever did. Except when I was one year old. I punched in the front of a celluloid rattle that was shaped like a baby's smiling face. I still have the rattle, and I hang it on my tree every Christmas as an ornament. It's there to remind me of my destructive tendencies."

"I don't think any of the rest of us need to be reminded," said Emerson tartly.

Everyone laughed. It was a wonderful sound, and Anthony was glad to join in.